ISBN 978-1-331-50323-1
PIBN 10198911

FB &c Ltd, Dalton House, 60 Windsor Avenue, London, SW19 2RR.
Company number 08720141. Registered in England and Wales.

For support please visit www.forgottenbooks.com

VOTES FOR WOMEN

A PLAY IN THREE ACTS

BY

ELIZABETH ROBINS

MILLS & BOON, LIMITED
49 WHITCOMB STREET
LONDON W.C.

[1909]

CAST

Lord John Wynnstay	
Lady John Wynnstay	*His wife*
Mrs. Heriot	*Sister of* Lady *John*
Miss Jean Dunbarton	*Niece to* Lady *John and Mrs. Heriot*
The Hon. Geoffrey Stonor ...	*Unionist M.P. affianced to Jean Dunbarton*
Mr. St. John Greatorex	L*iberal M.P.*
The Hon. Richard Farnborough	
Mr. Freddy Tunbridge	
Mrs. Freddy Tunbridge	
Mr. Allen Trent	
Miss Ernestine Blunt	*A Suffragette*
Mr. Pilcher	*A working man*
A Working Woman	
and	
Miss Vida Levering	

Persons in the Crowd: Servants in the Two Houses.

ACT I

Wynnstay House in Hertfordshire

ACT II

Trafalgar Square, London

ACT III

Eaton Square

(*Entire Action of Play takes place between Sunday* noon *and six o'clock in the evening of the same day.*)

ACT I.

THE HALL OF WYNNSTAY HOUSE.

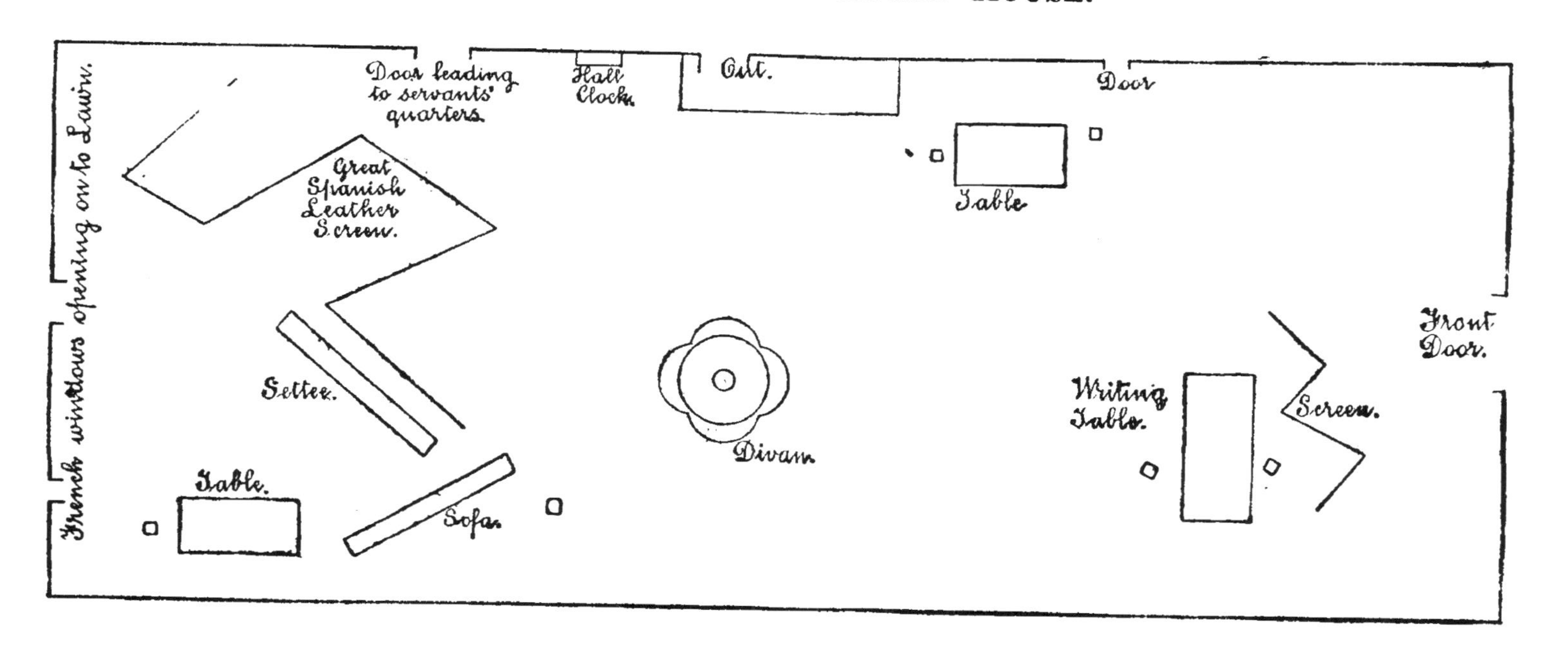

Twelve o'clock Sunday morning at end of June.
Action takes place between welve and six same day.

VOTES FOR WOMEN

ACT I

HALL OF WYNNSTAY HOUSE.

Twelve o'clock, Sunday morning, end of June. With the rising of the Curtain, enter the BUTLER. *As he is going, with majestic port, to answer the door* L., *enter briskly from the garden, by lower French window,* LADY JOHN WYNNSTAY, *flushed, and flapping a garden hat to fan herself. She is a pink-cheeked woman of fifty-four, who has plainly been a beauty, keeps her complexion, but is "gone to fat."*

LADY JOHN. Has Miss Levering come down yet?

BUTLER (*pausing* C.). I haven't seen her, m'lady.

LADY JOHN (*almost sharply as* BUTLER *turns* L.). I won't have her disturbed if she's resting. (*To herself as she goes to writing-table.*) She certainly needs it.

BUTLER. Yes, m'lady.

LADY JOHN (*sitting at writing-table, her back to front door*). But I want her to know the moment she comes down that the new plans arrived by the morning post.

BUTLER (*pausing nearly at the door*). Plans, m'la——

LADY JOHN. She'll understand. There they are.

B

(*Glancing at the clock.*) It's very important she should have them in time to look over before she goes——

(BUTLER *opens the door* L.)

(*Over her shoulder.*) Is that Miss Levering?

BUTLER. No, m'lady. Mr. Farnborough.

[*Exit* BUTLER.

(*Enter the* HON. R. FARNBOROUGH. *He is twenty-six; reddish hair, high-coloured, sanguine, self-important.*)

FARNBOROUGH. I'm afraid I'm scandalously early. It didn't take me nearly as long to motor over as Lord John said.

LADY JOHN (*shaking hands*). I'm afraid my husband is no authority on motoring—and he's not home yet from church.

FARN. It's the greatest luck finding *you*. I thought Miss Levering was the only person under this roof who was ever allowed to observe Sunday as a real Day of Rest.

LADY JOHN. If you've come to see Miss Levering——

FARN. Is she here? I give you my word I didn't know it.

LADY JOHN (*unconvinced*). Oh?

FARN. Does she come every week-end?

LADY JOHN. Whenever we can get her to. But we've only known her a couple of months.

FARN. And I have only known her three weeks! Lady John, I've come to ask you to help me.

LADY JOHN (*quickly*). With Miss Levering? I can't do it!

FARN. No, no—all that's no good. She only laughs.

LADY JOHN (*relieved*). Ah!—she looks upon you as a boy.

FARN (*firing up*). Such rot! What do you th*i*nk she said to me in London the other day?

LADY JOHN. That she was four years older than you?

FARN. Oh, I knew that. No. She sa*i*d she knew she was all the charm*i*ng things I'd been saying, but there was only one way to prove it—and that was to marry some one young enough to be her son. She'd noticed that was what the *most* attractive women did—and she named names.

LADY JOHN (*laughing*). *You* were too old!

FARN. (*nods*). Her future husband, she sa*i*d, was probably just entering Eton.

LADY JOHN. Just like her!

FARN. (*waving the subject away*). No. I wanted to see you about the Secretaryship.

LADY JOHN. You didn't get it, then?

FARN. No. It's the gr*i*ef of my l*i*fe.

LADY JOHN. Oh, *i*f you don't get one you'll get another.

FARN. But there *is* only one.

LADY JOHN. Only one vacancy?

FARN. Only one man I'd give my ears to work for.

LADY JOHN (*smiling*). I remember.

FARN. (*quickly*). Do I always talk about Stonor? Well, it's a habit people have got into.

LADY JOHN. I forget, do you know Mr. Stonor personally, or (*smiling*) are you just dazzled from afar?

FARN. Oh, I know him. The trouble is he doesn't know me. If he did he'd realise he can't be sure of winning his election without my valuable serv*i*ces.

LADY JOHN. Geoffrey Stonor's re-elect*i*on is always a foregone conclusion.

FARN. That the great man shares that opinion is precisely his weak point. (*Smiling.*) His only one.

LADY JOHN. You think because the Liberals swept the country the last time——

FARN. How can we be sure any Conservative seat is safe after——

(*As* LADY JOHN *smiles and turns to her papers.*) Forgive me, I know you're not interested in politics *qua* politics. But this concerns Geoffrey Stonor.

LADY JOHN. And you count on my being interested in him like all the rest of my sex.

FARN. (*leans forward*). Lady John, I've heard the news.

LADY JOHN. What news?

FARN. That your little niece—the Scotch heiress—is going to become Mrs. Geoffrey Stonor.

LADY JOHN. Who told you that?

FARN. Please don't mind my knowing.

LADY JOHN (*visibly perturbed*). She had set her heart upon having a few days with just her family in the secret, before the flood of congratulations breaks loose.

FARN. Oh, that's all right. I always hear things before other people.

LADY JOHN. Well, I must ask you to be good enough to be very circumspect. I wouldn't have my niece think that I——

FARN. Oh, of course not.

LADY JOHN. She will be here in an hour.

FARN. (*jumping up delighted*). What? To-day? The future Mrs. Stonor!

LADY JOHN (*harassed*). Yes. Unfortunately we had one or two people already asked for the week-end——

FARN. And I go and invite myself to luncheon! Lady John, you can buy me off. I'll promise to remove myself in five minutes if you'll——

LADY JOHN. No, the penalty is you shall stay and keep the others amused between church and luncheon, and so leave me free. (*Takes up the plan.*) Only *remember*——

FARN. Wild horses won't get a hint out of me! I only mentioned it to you because—since we've come back to live in this part of the world you've been so awfully kind—I thought, I hoped maybe you—you'd put in a word for me.

LADY JOHN. With——?

FARN. With your nephew that is to be. Though I'm *not* the slavish satellite people make out, you can't doubt——

LADY JOHN. Oh, I don't doubt. But you know Mr. Stonor inspires a similar enthusiasm in a good many young——

FARN. They haven't studied the situation as I have. They don't know what's at stake. They don't go to that hole Dutfield as I did just to hear his Friday speech.

LADY JOHN. Ah! But you were rewarded. Jean —my niece—wrote me it was "glorious."

FARN. (*judicially*). Well, you know, *I* was disappointed. He's too content just to criticise, just to make his delicate pungent fun of the men who are grappling—very inadequately, of course—still *grappling* with the big questions. There's a carrying power (*gets up and faces an imaginary audience*)—some of Stonor's friends ought to point it out—there's a driving power in the poorest constructive policy that makes the most brilliant criticism look barren.

LADY JOHN (*with good-humoured malice*). Who told you that?

FARN. You think there's nothing *in* it because *I* say it. But now that he's coming into the family, Lord John or somebody really ought to point out— Stonor's overdoing his rôle of magnificent security.

LADY JOHN. I don't see even Lord John offering to instruct Mr. Stonor.

FARN. Believe me, that's just Stonor's danger! Nobody saying a word, everybody hoping he's on the point of adopting some definite line, something strong and original that's going to fire the public imagination and bring the Tories back into power.

LADY JOHN. So he will.

FARN. (*hotly*). Not if he disappoints meetings— goes calmly up to town—and leaves the field to the Liberals.

LADY JOHN. When did he do anything like that?

FARN. Yesterday! (*With a harassed air.*) And now that he's got this other preoccupation——

LADY JOHN. You mean——

FARN. Yes, your niece—that spoilt child of Fortune. Of course! (*Stopping suddenly.*) She kept him from the meeting last night. Well! (*sits down*) if that's the effect she's going to have it's pretty serious!

LADY JOHN (*smiling*). *You* are!

FARN. I can assure you the election agent's more so. He's simply tearing his hair.

LADY JOHN (*more gravely and coming nearer*). How do you know?

FARN. He told me so himself—yesterday. I scraped acquaintance with the agent just to see if—if——

LADY JOHN. It's not only here that you manœuvre for that Secretaryship!

FARN. (*confidentially*). You can never tell when your chance might come! That election chap's promised to keep me posted.

(*The door flies open and* JEAN DUNBARTON *rushes in.*)

JEAN. Aunt Ellen—here I——

LADY JOHN (*astonished*). My dear child!

(*They embrace. Enter* LORD JOHN *from the garden—a benevolent, silver-haired despot of sixty-two.*)

LORD JOHN. I thought that was you running up the avenue.

(JEAN *greets her uncle warmly, but all the time she and her aunt talk together.* "*How did you get here so early?*" "*I knew you'd be surprised—wasn't it clever of me to manage it? I don't deserve all the credit.*" "*But there isn't any train between——*" "*Yes, wait till I tell you.*" "*You walked in the broiling sun——*" "*No, no.*" "*You must be dead. Why didn't you telegraph? I ordered the carriage to meet the* 1.10. *Didn't you say the* 1.10? *Yes, I'm sure you did—here's your letter.*")

LORD J. (*has shaken hands with* FARNBOROUGH *and speaks through the torrent*). Now they'll tell each other for ten minutes that she's an hour earlier than we expected.

(LORD JOHN *leads* FARNBOROUGH *towards the garden.*)

FARN. The Freddy Tunbridges said *they* were coming to you this week.

LORD J. Yes, they're dawdling through the park with the Church Brigade.

FARN. Oh! (*With a glance back at* JEAN.) I'll go and meet them.

[*Exit* FARNBOROUGH.

LORD J. (*as he turns back*). That discreet young man will get on.

LADY JOHN (*to* JEAN). But *how* did you get here?

JEAN (*breathless*). "He" motored me down.

LADY JOHN. Geoffrey Stonor? (JEAN *nods.*) Why, where is he, then?

JEAN. He dropped me at the end of the avenue and went on to see a supporter about something.

LORD J. You let him go off like that without——

LADY JOHN (*taking* JEAN'S *two hands*). Just tell me, my child, is it all right?

JEAN. My engagement? (*Radiantly.*) Yes, absolutely.

LADY JOHN. Geoffrey Stonor *isn't* going to be—a little too old for you?

JEAN (*laughing*). Bless me, am I such a chicken?

LADY JOHN. Twenty-four used not to be so young—but it's become so.

JEAN. Yes, we don't grow up so quick. (*Gaily.*) But on the other hand we *stay* up longer.

LORD J. You've got what's vulgarly called "looks," my dear, and that will help to *keep* you up!

JEAN (*smiling*). I know what Uncle John's thinking. But I'm not the only girl who's been left "what's vulgarly called" money.

LORD J. You're the only one of our immediate circle who's been left so beautifully much.

JEAN. Ah, but remember Geoffrey could—everybody *knows* he could have married any one in England.

LADY JOHN (*faintly ironic*). I'm afraid everybody does know it—not excepting Mr. Stonor.

LORD J. Well, how spoilt is the great man?

JEAN. Not the least little bit in the world. You'll see! He so wants to know my best-beloved relations better. (*Another embrace.*) An orphan has so few belongings, she has to make the most of them.

LORD J. (*smiling*). Let us hope he'll approve of us on more intimate acquaintance.

JEAN (*firmly*). He will. He's an angel. Why, he gets on with my grandfather!

LADY JOHN. *Does* he? (*Teasing.*) You mean to say Mr. Geoffrey Stonor isn't just a tiny bit—"superior" about Dissenters.

JEAN (*stoutly*). Not half as much as Uncle John and all the rest of you! My grandfather's been ill again, you know, and rather difficult—bless him! (*Radiantly.*) But Geoffrey—— (*Clasps her hands.*)

LADY JOHN. He must have powers of persuasion! —to get that old Covenanter to let you come in an abhorred motor-car—on Sunday, too!

JEAN (*half whispering*). Grandfather didn't know!

LADY JOHN. Didn't know?

JEAN. I honestly meant to come by train. Geoffrey met me on my way to the station. We had the most glorious run. Oh, Aunt Ellen, we're so happy! (*Embracing her.*) I've so looked forward to having you to myself the whole day just to talk to you about——

LORD J. (*turning away with affected displeasure*). Oh, very well——

JEAN (*catches him affectionately by the arm*). *You'd* find it dreffly dull to hear me talk about Geoffrey the whole blessed day!

LADY JOHN. Well, till luncheon, my dear, you

mustn't mind if I—— (*To* LORD JOHN, *as she goes to writing-table.*) Miss Levering wasn't only tired last night, she was ill.

LORD J. I thought she looked very white.

JEAN. Who is Miss —— You don't mean to say there are other people ?

LADY JOHN. One or two. Your uncle's responsible for asking that old cynic, St. John Greatorex, and I——

JEAN (*gravely*). Mr. Greatorex—he's a Rad*i*cal, *i*sn't he ?

LORD J. (*laughing*). *Jean !* Beg*i*nn*i*ng to "think in parties" !

LADY JOHN. It's very natural now that she should——

JEAN. I only meant it was odd he should be here. Naturally at my grandfather's——

LORD J. It's all r*i*ght, my child. Of course we expect now that you'll begin to think like Geoffrey Stonor, and to feel like Geoffrey Stonor, and to talk like Geoffrey Stonor. And quite proper too.

JEAN (*smiling*). Well, if I do think with my husband and feel with him—as, of course, I shall—it will surprise me if I ever find myself talking a tenth as well——

(*Following her uncle to the French window.*)

You should have heard him at Dutfield—— (*Stopping short, delighted.*) Oh ! The Freddy Tunbridges. What ? Not Aunt Lydia ! Oh-h !

(*Looking back reproachfully at* LADY JOHN, *who makes a discreet motion* "*I couldn't help it.*")

(*Enter the* TUNBRIDGES. MR. FREDDY, *of no profession and of independent means. Well-groomed, pleasant-looking ; of few words. A "nice man" who likes "nice women," and has married one of them.* MRS. FREDDY *is thirty. An attractive figure, delicate face, intelligent grey eyes, over-sensitive mouth, and naturally curling dust-coloured hair.*)

MRS. FREDDY. What a delightful surprise!

JEAN (*shaking hands warmly*). I'm so glad. How d'ye do, Mr. Freddy?

(*Enter* LADY JOHN'S *sister*, MRS. HERIOT—*smart, pompous, fifty—followed by* FARNBOROUGH.)

MRS. HERIOT. My dear Jean! My darling child!

JEAN. How do you do, aunt?

MRS. H. (*sotto voce*). *I* wasn't surprised. I always prophesied——

JEAN. Sh! *Please!*

FARN. We haven't met since you were in short skirts. I'm Dick Farnborough.

JEAN. Oh, I remember.

(*They shake hands.*)

MRS. F. (*looking round*). Not down yet—the Elusive One?

JEAN. Who is the Elusive One?

MRS. F. Lady John's new friend.

LORD J. (*to* JEAN). Oh, I forgot you hadn't seen Miss Levering; such a nice creature! (*To* MRS. FREDDY.) —don't you think?

MRS. F. Of course I do. You're lucky to get her to come so often. She won't go to other people.

LADY JOHN. She knows she can rest here.

FREDDY (*who has joined* LADY JOHN *near the writing-table*). What does she do to tire her?

LADY JOHN. She's been helping my *sister* and me with a scheme of ours.

MRS. H. She certainly knows how to inveigle money out of the men.

LADY JOHN. It would sound less equ*i*vocal, Lydia, if you added that the money is to bu*i*ld baths in our Shelter for Homeless Women.

MRS. F. Homeless women ?

LADY JOHN. Yes, in the most *i*nsanitary part of Soho.

FREDDY. Oh—a—really.

FARN. It doesn't sound quite in Miss Levering's line!

LADY JOHN. My dear boy, you know as l*i*ttle about what's in a woman's line as most men.

FREDDY (*laughing*). Oh, I say!

LORD J. (*indulgently to* MR. FREDDY *and* FARNBOROUGH). Philanthropy in a woman like Miss Levering is a form of restlessness. But she's a *nice* creature; all she needs is to get some "nice" fella to marry her.

MRS. F. (*laughing as she hangs on her husband's arm*). Yes, a woman needs a balance wheel—if only to keep her from flying back to town on a hot day like this.

LORD J. Who's proposing anything so——

MRS. F. The Elus*i*ve One.

LORD J. Not Miss——

MRS. F. Yes, before luncheon!

[*Exit* FARNBOROUGH *to garden.*

LADY JOHN. She must be in London by this afternoon, she says.

LORD J. What for in the name of——

LADY JOHN. Well, *that* I didn't ask her. But (*consults watch*) I think I'll just go up and see if she's changed her plans.

[*Exit* LADY JOHN.

LORD J. Oh, she must be *made* to. Such a nice creature! All she needs——

(*Voices outside. Enter fussily, talking and gesticulating,* ST. JOHN GREATOREX, *followed by* MISS LEVERING *and* FARNBOROUGH. GREATOREX *is sixty, wealthy, a county magnate, and Liberal M.P. He is square, thick-set, square-bearded. His shining bald pate has two strands of coal-black hair trained across his crown from left ear to right and securely pasted there. He has small, twinkling eyes and a reputation for telling good stories after dinner when ladies have left the room. He is carrying a little book for* MISS LEVERING. *She (parasol over shoulder), an attractive, essentially feminine, and rather "smart" woman of thirty-two, with a somewhat foreign grace; the kind of whom men and women alike say, "What's her story? Why doesn't she marry?"*)

GREATOREX. I protest! Good Lord! what are the women of this country coming to? I *protest* against Miss Levering being carried off to discuss anything so revolting. Bless my soul! what can a woman like you *know* about it?

MISS LEVERING (*smiling*). Little enough. Good morning.

GREAT. (*relieved*). I should think so indeed!

LORD J. (*aside*). You aren't serious about going——

GREAT. (*waggishly breaking in*). We were so happy out there in the summer-house, weren't we?

MISS L. Ideally.

GREAT. And to be haled out to talk about Public *Sanitation* forsooth!

(*Hurries after* MISS LEVERING *as she advances to speak to the* FREDDYS, *&c.*)

Why, God bless my soul, do you realise that's *drains?*

MISS L. I'm dreadfully afraid it is! (*Holds out her hand for the small book* GREATOREX *is carrying.*)

(GREATOREX *returns* MISS LEVERING'S *book open; he has been keeping the place with his finger. She opens it and shuts her handkerchief in.*)

GREAT. And we in the act of discussing Italian literature! Perhaps you'll tell me that isn't a more savoury topic for a lady.

MISS L. But for the tramp population less conducive to savouriness, don't you think, than—baths?

GREAT. No, I can't understand this morbid interest in vagrants. *You're* much too—leave it to the others.

JEAN. What others?

GREAT. (*with smiling impertinence*). Oh, the sort of woman who smells of indiarubber. The typical English spinster. (*To* MISS LEVERING.) *You* know—Italy's full of her. She never goes anywhere without a mackintosh and a collapsible bath—rubber. When you look at her, it's borne in upon you that she doesn't only smell of rubber. *She's* rubber too.

LORD J. (*laughing*). This is my niece, Miss Jean Dunbarton, Miss Levering.

JEAN. How do you do? (*They shake hands.*)

GREAT. (*to* JEAN). I'm sure *you* agree with me.

JEAN. About Miss Levering being too——

GREAT. For that sort of thing—*much* too——

MISS L. What a pity you've exhausted the more eloquent adjectives.

GREAT. But I haven't!

MISS L. Well, you can't say to me as you did to Mrs. Freddy: "You're too young and too happily married—and too——

(*Glances round smiling at* MRS. FREDDY, *who, oblivious, is laughing and talking to her husband and* MRS. HERIOT.)

JEAN. For what was Mrs. Freddy too happily married and all the rest?

MISS L. (*lightly*). Mr. Greatorex was repudiating the horrid rumour that Mrs. Freddy had been speaking in public; about Women's Trade Unions—wasn't that what you said, Mrs. Heriot?

LORD J. (*chuckling*). Yes, it isn't made up as carefully as your aunt's parties usually are. Here we've got Greatorex (*takes his arm*) who hates political women, and we've got in that mild and inoffensive-looking little lady——

(*Motion over his shoulder towards* MRS. FREDDY.)

GREAT. (*shrinking down stage in comic terror*). You don't mean she's *really*——

JEAN (*simultaneously and gaily rising*). Oh, and you've got me!

LORD J. (*with genial affection*). My dear child, he doesn't hate the charming wives and sweethearts who help to win seats.

(JEAN *makes her uncle a discreet little signal of warning.*)

MISS L. Mr. Greatorex objects only to the unsexed creatures who—a——

LORD J. (*hastily to cover up his slip*). Yes, yes, who want to act independently of men.

MISS L. Vote, and do silly things of that sort.

LORD J. (*with enthusiasm*). Exactly.

MRS. H. It will be a long time before we hear any more of *that* nonsense.

JEAN. You mean that rowdy scene in the House of Commons?

MRS. H. Yes. No decent woman will be able to say "Suffrage" without blushing for another generation, thank Heaven!

MISS L. (*smiling*). Oh? I understood that so little I almost imagined people were more stirred up about it than they'd ever been before.

GREAT. (*with a quizzical affectation of gallantry*). Not people like you.

MISS L. (*teasingly*). How do you know?

GREAT. (*with a start*). God bless my soul!

LORD J. She's saying that only to get a rise out of you.

GREAT. Ah, yes, your frocks aren't serious enough.

MISS L. I'm told it's an exploded notion that the Suffrage women are all dowdy and dull.

GREAT. Don't you believe it!

MISS L. Well, of course we know you've been an authority on the subject for—let's see, how many years is it you've kept the House in roars whenever Woman's Rights are mentioned?

GREAT. (*flattered but not entirely comfortable*). Oh, as long as I've known anything about politics there have been a few discontented old maids and hungry widows——

MISS L. "A few!" That's really rather forbearing of you, Mr. Greatorex. I'm afraid the number of the discontented and the hungry was 96,000—among the mill operat*i*ves alone. (*Hastily.*) At least the papers sa*i*d so, didn't they?

GREAT. Oh, don't ask me; that kind of woman doesn't interest me, I'm afraid. Only I am able to point out to the people who lose their heads and seem inclined to treat the phenomenon seriously that there's absolutely nothing new in it. There have been women for the last forty years who haven't had anyth*i*ng more pressing to do than petition Parliament.

MISS L. (*reflectively*). And that's as far as they've got.

LORD J. (*turning on his heel*). It's as far as they'll ever get.

(*Meets the group up* R. *coming down.*)

MISS L. (*chaffing* GREATOREX). Let me see, wasn't a deputation sent to you not long ago? (*Sits* C.)

GREAT. H'm! (*Irritably.*) Yes, yes.

MISS L. (*as though she has just recalled the circumstances*). Oh, yes, I remember. I thought at the t*i*me, *i*n my modest way, it was nothing short of heroic of them to go asking audience of their arch opponent.

GREAT. (*stoutly*). It didn't come off.

MISS L. (*innocently*). Oh! I thought they insisted on bearding the lion in his den.

GREAT. Of course I wasn't go*i*ng to be bothered with a lot of——

MISS L. You don't mean you refused to go out and face them!

GREAT. (*with a comic look of terror*). I wouldn't have done it for worlds. But a fr*i*end of m*i*ne went and had a look at 'em.

MISS L. (*smiling*). Well, did he get back al*i*ve?

GREAT. Yes, but he advised me not to go. "You're quite right," he said. "Don't you think of bothering," he said. "I've looked over the lot," he said, "and there isn't a week-ender among 'em."

JEAN (*gaily precipitates herself into the conversation*). You remember Mrs. Freddy's friend who came to tea here in the winter? (*To* GREATOREX.) He was a member of Parliament too—quite a little young one—he said women would never be respected till they had the vote!

(GREATOREX *snorts, the other men smile and all the women except* MRS. HERIOT.)

MRS. H. (*sniffing*). I remember telling him that he was too young to know what he was talking about.

LORD J. Yes, I'm afraid you all sat on the poor gentleman.

LADY JOHN (*entering*). Oh, *there* you are!

(*Greets* MISS LEVERING.)

JEAN. It was such fun. He was flat as a pancake when we'd done with him. Aunt Ellen told him with her most distinguished air she didn't want to be "respected."

MRS. F. (*with a little laugh of remonstrance*). My *dear* Lady John!

FARN. Quite right! Awful idea to think you're *respected!*

MISS L. (*smiling*). Simply revolting.

LADY JOHN (*at writing-table*). Now, you frivolous people, go away. We've only got a few minutes to talk over the terms of the late Mr. Soper's munificence before the carriage comes for Miss Levering——

MRS. F. (*to* FARNBOROUGH). Did you know she'd

got that old horror to give Lady John £8,000 for her charity before he died?

MRS. F. Who got him to?

LADY JOHN. Miss Levering. He wouldn't do it for me, but she brought him round.

FREDDY. Yes. Bah-ee Jove! I expect so.

MRS. F. (*turning enthusiastically to her husband*). Isn't she wonderful?

LORD J. (*aside*). Nice creature. All she needs is——

(MR. *and* MRS. FREDDY *and* FARNBOROUGH *stroll off to the garden.* LADY JOHN *on far side of the writing-table.* MRS. HERIOT *at the top.* JEAN *and* LORD JOHN, L.)

GREAT. (*on divan* C., *aside to* MISS LEVERING). Too "wonderful" to waste your time on the wrong people.

MISS L. I shall waste less of my time after this.

GREAT. I'm relieved to hear it. I can't see you wheedling money for shelters and rot of that sort out of retired grocers.

MISS L. You see, you call it rot. We couldn't have got £8,000 out of *you*.

GREAT. (*very low*). I'm not sure.

(MISS LEVERING *looks at him.*)

GREAT. If I gave you that much—for your little projects—what would you give me?

MISS L. (*speaking quietly*). Soper didn't ask that.

GREAT. (*horrified*). Soper! I should think not!

LORD J. (*turning to* MISS LEVERING). Soper? You two still talking Soper? How flattered the old beggar'd be!

LORD J. (*lower*). Did you hear what Mrs. Heriot said about him? "So kind; so munificent—so *vulgar*, poor soul, we couldn't know him in London—*but we shall meet him in heaven.*"

(GREATOREX *and* LORD JOHN *go off laughing.*)

LADY JOHN (*to Miss Levering*). Sit over there, my dear. (*Indicating chair in front of writing-table.*) You needn't stay, Jean. This won't interest you.

MISS L. (*in the tone of one agreeing*). It's only an effort to meet the greatest evil in the world?

JEAN (*pausing as she's following the others*). What do you call the greatest evil in the world?

(*Looks pass between* MRS. HERIOT *and* LADY JOHN.)

MISS L. (*without emphasis*). The helplessness of women.

(JEAN *stands still.*)

LADY JOHN (*rising and putting her arm about the girl's shoulder*). Jean, darling, I know you can think of nothing but (*aside*) *him*—so just go and——

JEAN (*brightly*). Indeed, indeed, I can think of every*thing* better than I ever did before. He has lit up everything for me—made everything *v*ivider, more —more significant.

MISS L. (*turning round*). Who has?

JEAN. Oh, yes, I don't care about other things less but a thousand times more.

LADY JOHN. You *are* in love.

MISS L. Oh, that's it! (*Smiling at* JEAN.) I congratulate you.

LADY JOHN (*returning to the outspread plan*). Well—*this*, you see, obv*i*ates the d*i*fficulty you raised.

MISS L. Yes, quite.

MRS. H. But it's going to cost a great deal more.

MISS L. It's worth it.

MRS. H. We'll have nothing left for the organ at St. Pilgrim's.

LADY JOHN. My dear Lydia, we're putting the organ aside.

MRS. H. (*with asperity*). We can't afford to "put aside" the elevating effect of music.

LADY JOHN. What we must make for, first, is the cheap and humanely conducted lodging-house.

MRS. H. There are several of those already, but poor St. Pilgrim's——

MISS L. There are none for the poorest women.

LADY JOHN. No, even the excellent Soper was for multiplying Rowton Houses. You can never get men to realise—you can't always get women——

MISS L. It's the work least able to wait.

MRS. H. I don't agree with you, and I happen to have spent a great deal of my life in works of charity.

MISS L. Ah, then you'll be interested in the girl I saw dying in a Tramp Ward a little while ago. *Glad* her cough was worse—only she mustn't die before her father. Two reasons. Nobody but her to keep the old man out of the workhouse—and "father is so proud." If she died first, he would starve ; worst of all he might hear what had happened up in London to his girl.

MRS. H. She didn't say, I suppose, how she happened to fall so low.

MISS L. Yes, she had been *in* service. She lost the train back one Sunday night and was too terrified of her employer to dare *ring* him up after hours. The wrong person found her crying on the platform.

MRS. H. She should have gone to one of the Friendly Societies.

MISS L. At eleven at night?

MRS. H. And there are the Rescue Leagues. I myself have been connected with one for twenty years——

MISS L. (*reflectively*). "Twenty years!" Always arriving "after the train's gone"—after the girl and the Wrong Person have got to the journey's end.

(MRS. HERIOT'S *eyes flash.*)

JEAN. Where is she now?

LADY JOHN. Never m*i*nd.

MISS L. Two n*i*ghts ago she was waiting at a street corner in the rain.

MRS. H. Near a publ*i*c-house, I suppose.

MISS L. Yes, a sort of "public-house." She was plainly dy*i*ng—she was told she shouldn't be out in the rain. "I mustn't go in yet," she said. "*This* is what he gave me," and she began to cry. In her hand were two pennies silvered over to look like half-crowns.

MRS. H. I don't believe that story. It's just the sort of thing some sensation-monger trumps up—now, who tells you such ——

MISS L. Several credible people. I d*i*dn't be-l*i*eve them till ——

JEAN. Till ——?

MISS L. Till last week I saw for myself.

LADY JOHN. *Saw?* Where?

MISS L In a low lodging-house not a hundred yards from the church you want a new organ for.

MRS. H. How did *you* happen to be there?

MISS L. I was on a pilgrimage.

JEAN. A pilgrimage?

MISS L. Into the Underworld.

LADY JOHN. *You* went?

JEAN. How *could* you?

MISS L. I put on an old gown and a tawdry hat—— (*Turns to* LADY JOHN.) You'll never know how many things are hidden from a woman in good clothes. The bold, free look of a man at a woman he believes to be destitute—you must *feel* that look on you before you can understand—a good half of history.

MRS. H. (*rises*). Jean !——

JEAN. But where did you go—dressed like that ?

MISS L. Down among the homeless women—on a wet night looking for shelter.

LADY JOHN (*hastily*). No wonder you've been ill.

JEAN (*under breath*). And it's like that ?

MISS L. No.

JEAN. No ?

MISS L. It's so much worse I dare not tell about it —even if you weren't here I couldn't.

MRS. H. (*to* JEAN). You needn't suppose, darling, that those wretched creatures feel it as we would.

MISS L. The girls who need shelter and work aren't all serving-maids.

MRS. H. (*with an involuntary flash*). We know that all the women who—*make mistakes* aren't.

MISS L. (*steadily*). That is why *every* woman ought to take an interest in this—every girl too.

JEAN } (*simultaneously*) { Yes—oh, yes !
LADY JOHN } (*simultaneously*) { No. This is a matter for us older——

MRS. H. (*with an air of sly challenge*). Or for a person who has some special knowledge. (*Significantly.*) *We* can't pretend to have access to such sources of information as Miss Levering.

MISS L. (*meeting* MRS. HERIOT'S *eye steadily*). Yes, for I can give you access. As you seem to think, I have some first-hand knowledge about homeless girls.

LADY JOHN (*cheerfully turning it aside*). Well, my dear, it will all come in convenient. (*Tapping the plan.*)

MISS L. It once happened to me to take offence at an ugly thing that was going on under my father's roof. Oh, *years* ago! I was an impulsive girl. I turned my back on my father's house——

LADY JOHN (*for* JEAN'S *benefit*). That was ill-advised.

MRS. H. Of course, if a girl does *that*——

MISS L. That was what all my relations said (*with a glance at* JEAN), and I couldn't explain.

JEAN. Not to your mother?

MISS L. She was dead. I went to London to a small hotel and tried to find employment. I wandered about all day and every day from agency to agency. I was supposed to be educated. I'd been brought up partly in Paris; I could play several instruments, and sing little songs in four different tongues. (*Slight pause.*)

JEAN. Did nobody want you to teach French or sing the little songs?

MISS L. The heads of schools thought me too young. There were people ready to listen to my singing, but the terms—they were too hard. Soon my money was gone. I began to pawn my trinkets. *They* went.

JEAN. And still no work?

MISS L. No; but by that time I had some real education—an unpaid hotel bill, and not a shilling in the world. (*Slight pause.*) Some girls think it hardship to have to earn their living. The horror is not to be allowed to——

JEAN. (*bending forward*). What happened?

LADY JOHN (*rises*). My dear (*to* MISS LEVERING), have your things been sent down? Are you quite ready?

MISS L. Yes, all but my hat.

JEAN. Well?

MISS L. Well, by chance I met a friend of my family.

JEAN. That was lucky.

MISS L. I thought so. He was nearly ten years older than I. He said he wanted to help me. (*Pause.*)

JEAN. And didn't he?

(LADY JOHN *lays her hand on* MISS LEVERING'S *shoulder.*)

MISS L. Perhaps after all he did. (*With sudden change of tone.*) Why do I waste time over myself? I belonged to the little class of armed women. My body wasn't born weak, and my spirit wasn't broken by the *habit* of slavery. But, as Mrs. Heriot was kind enough to hint, I do know something about the possible fate of homeless girls. I found there were pleasant parks, museums, free libraries in our great rich London—and not one single place where destitute women can be sure of work that *isn't* killing or food that isn't worse than prison fare. That's why women ought not to sleep o' nights till this Shelter stands spreading out wide arms.

JEAN. No, no——

MRS. H. (*gathering up her gloves, fan, prayer-book, &c.*). Even when it's *built*—you'll see! Many of those creatures will prefer the *life* they lead. They *like* it.

MISS L. A woman told me—one of the sort that

knows—told me many of them "like it" so much that they are indifferent to the risk of being sent to prison. "*It gives them a rest*," she said.

LADY JOHN. A rest!

(MISS LEVERING *glances at the clock as she rises to go upstairs.*)

(LADY JOHN *and* MRS. HERIOT *bend their heads over the plan, covertly talking.*)

JEAN (*intercepting* MISS LEVERING). I want to begin to understand something of—I'm horribly ignorant.

MISS L. (*Looks at her searchingly*). I'm a rather busy person——

JEAN. (*interrupting*). I have a quite special reason for wanting *not* to be ignorant. (*Impulsively*). I'll go to town to-morrow, if you'll come and lunch with me.

MISS L. Thank you—I (*catches* MRS. HERIOT'S *eye*)—I must go and put my hat on.

[*Exit upstairs.*

MRS. H. (*aside*). How little she minds all these horrors!

LADY JOHN. They turn me cold. Ugh! (*Rising, harassed.*) I wonder if she's signed the visitors' book!

MRS. H. For all her Shelter schemes, she's a hard woman.

JEAN. Miss Levering is?

MRS. H. Oh, of course *you* won't think so. She has angled very adroitly for your sympathy.

JEAN. She doesn't look hard.

LADY JOHN (*glancing at* JEAN *and taking alarm*). I'm not sure but what she does. Her mouth—always like this . . . as *if* she were hold*ing* back someth*ing* by main force!

MRS. H. (*half under her breath*). Well, so she is.

[*Exit* LADY JOHN *into the lobby to look at the visitors' book.*

JEAN. Why haven't I seen her before?

MRS. H. Oh, she's lived abroad. (*Debating with herself.*) You don't know about her, I suppose?

JEAN. I don't know how Aunt Ellen came to know her.

MRS. H. That was my doing. But I didn't barga*i*n for her being introduced to you.

JEAN. She seems to go everywhere. And why shouldn't she?

MRS. H. (*quickly*). You mustn't ask her to Eaton Square.

JEAN. I have.

MRS. H. Then you'll have to get out of it.

JEAN (*with a stubborn look*). I must have a reason. And a very good reason.

MRS. H. Well, it's not a thing I should have preferred to tell you, but I know how difficult you are to guide . . . so I suppose you'll have to know. (*Lowering her voice.*) It was ten or twelve years ago. I found her horribly ill in a lonely Welsh farmhouse. We had taken the Manor for that August. The farmer's w*i*fe was frightened, and begged me to go and see what I thought. I soon saw how it was—I thought she was dying.

JEAN. *Dying!* What was the——

MRS. H. I got no more out of her than the farmer's wife did. She had had no letters. There had been no one to see her except a man down from London, a shady-looking doctor—nameless, of course. And then this result. The farmer and his wife, highly respectable people, were incensed. They were for turning the girl out.

JEAN. *Oh!* but——

MRS. H. Yes. Pitiless some of these people are! I insisted they should treat the girl humanely, and we became friends . . . that is, "sort of." In spite of all I did for her——

JEAN. What did you do?

MRS. H. I—I've told you, and I lent her money. No small sum either.

JEAN. Has she never paid it back?

MRS. H. Oh, yes, after a time. But I *always* kept her secret—as much as I knew of it.

JEAN. But you've been telling me!

MRS. H. That was my duty—and I *never* had her full confidence.

JEAN. Wasn't it natural she——

MRS. H. Well, all things considered, she might have wanted to tell me who was responsible.

JEAN. Oh! Aunt Lydia!

MRS. H. All she ever said was that she was ashamed —(*losing her temper and her fine feeling for the innocence of her auditor*)—ashamed that she "hadn't had the courage to resist"—not the original temptation but the pressure brought to bear on her "not to go through with it," as she said.

JEAN (*wrinkling her brows*). You are being so delicate—I'm not sure I understand.

MRS. H. (*irritably*). The only thing you need understand is that she's not a desirable companion for a young girl.

(*Pause.*)

JEAN. When did you see her after—after——

MRS. H. (*with a slight grimace*). I met her last winter at the Bishop's. (*Hurriedly.*) She's a connection of his wife's. They'd got her to help with some of their work. Then she took hold of ours. Your aunt and uncle are quite foolish about her, and I'm debarred from taking any steps, at least till the Shelter is out of hand.

JEAN. I do rather wonder she can bring herself to talk about—the unfortunate women of the world.

MRS. H. The effrontery of it!

JEAN. Or . . the courage! (*Puts her hand up to her throat as if the sentence had caught there.*)

MRS. H. Even presumes to set *me* right! Of course I don't *mind* in the least, poor soul but I feel I owe it to your dead mother to tell you about her, especially as you're old enough now to know something about life——

JEAN (*slowly*)—and since a girl needn't be very old to suffer for her ignorance. (*Moves a little away.*) I *felt* she was rather wonderful.

MRS. H. *Wonderful!*

JEAN (*pausing*). . . . To have lived through *that* when she was . . . how old?

MRS. H. (*rising*). Oh, nineteen or thereabouts.

JEAN. Five years younger than I. To be abandoned and to come out of it like this!

MRS. H. (*laying her hand on the girl's shoulder*). It was too bad to have to tell you such a sordid story to-day of all days.

JEAN. It is a very terrible story, but this wasn't a bad time. I feel very sorry to-day for women who aren't happy.

(*Motor horn heard faintly.*)

(*Jumping up.*) That's Geoffrey!

MRS. H. Mr. Stonor! What makes you think . . . ?

JEAN. Yes, yes. I'm sure, I'm sure——

(*Checks herself as she is flying off. Turns and sees* LORD JOHN *entering from the garden.*)

(*Motor horn louder.*)

LORD J. Who do you think is motoring up the drive?

JEAN (*catching hold of him*). Oh, dear! how am I ever going to be able to behave like a girl who isn't engaged to the only man in the world worth marrying?

MRS. H. You were expecting Mr. Stonor all the time!

JEAN. He promised he'd come to luncheon if it was humanly possible; but I was afraid to tell you for fear he'd be prevented.

LORD J. (*laughing as he crosses to the lobby*). You felt we couldn't have borne the disappointment.

JEAN. I felt I couldn't.

(*The lobby door opens.* LADY JOHN *appears radiant, followed by a tall figure in a dust-coat, &c., no goggles. He has straight, firm features, a little blunt; fair skin, high-coloured; fine, straight hair, very fair; grey eyes, set somewhat prominently and heavy when not interested; lips full, but firmly moulded.* GEOFFREY STONOR *is heavier than a man of forty should be, but otherwise in the pink of physical condition. The* FOOTMAN *stands waiting to help him off with his motor coat.*)

LADY JOHN. Here's an agreeable surprise!

(JEAN *has gone forward only a step, and stands smiling at the approaching figure.*)

LORD J. How do you do? (*As he comes between them and briskly shakes hands with* STONOR.)

(FARNBOROUGH *appears at the French window.*)

FARN. Yes, by Jove! *Turning to the others clustered round the window.*) What gigantic luck!

(*Those outside crane and glance, and then elaborately turn their backs and pretend to be talking among themselves, but betray as far as manners permit the enormous sensation the arrival has created.*)

STONOR. How do you do?

(*Shakes hands with* MRS. HERIOT, *who has rushed up to him with both hers outstretched. He crosses to* JEAN, *who meets him half way; they shake hands, smiling into each other's eyes.*)

JEAN. Such a long time since we met!

LORD J. (*to* STONOR). You're growing very enterprising. I could hardly believe my ears when I heard you'd motored all the way from town to see a supporter on Sunday.

STONOR. I don't know how we covered the ground in the old days. (*To* LADY JOHN.) It's no use to stand for your borough any more. The American, you know, he "runs" for Congress. By and by we shall all be flying after the thing we want.

(*Smiles at* JEAN.)

JEAN. Sh! (*Smiles and then glances over her shoulder and speaks low.*) All sorts of irrelevant people here.

FARN. (*unable to resist the temptation, comes forward*). How do you do, Mr. Stonor?

STONOR. Oh—how d'you do.

FARN. Some of them were arguing in the smoking-room last night whether it didn't hurt a man's chances going about in a motor.

LORD J. Yes, we've been hearing a lot of stories about the unpopularity of motor-cars—among the class that hasn't got 'em, of course. What do you say?

LADY JOHN. I'm sure you gain more votes by being able to reach so many more of your constituency than we used——

STONOR. Well, I don't know—I've sometimes wondered whether the charm of our presence wasn't counterbalanced by the way we tear about smothering our fellow-beings in dust and running down their pigs and chickens, not to speak of their children.

LORD J. (*anxiously*). What on the whole are the prospects?

(FARNBOROUGH *cranes forward.*)

STONOR (*gravely*). We shall have to work harder than we realised.

FARN. Ah!

(*Retires towards group.*)

JEAN (*in a half-aside as she slips her arm in her uncle's and smiles at* GEOFFREY). He says he believes I'll be able to make a real difference to his chances. Isn't it angelic of him?

STONOR (*in a jocular tone*). Angelic? Macchiavelian. I pin all my hopes on your being able to counteract the pernicious influence of my opponent's glib wife.

JEAN. You want me to have a *real* share in it all, don't you, Geoffrey?

STONOR (*smiling into her eyes*). Of course I do.

(FARNBOROUGH *drops down again on pretence of talking to* MRS. HERIOT.)

LORD J. I don't gather you're altogether sanguine. Any complication?

(JEAN *and* LADY JOHN *stand close together* (C.), *the girl radiant, following* STONOR *with her eyes and whispering to the sympathetic elder woman.*)

STONOR. Well (*taking Sunday paper out of pocket*), there's this agitation about the Woman Question. Oddly enough, it seems likely to affect the issue.

LORD J. Why should it? Can't you do what the other four hundred have done?

STONOR (*laughs*). Easily. But, you see, the mere fact that four hundred and twenty members have been worried into promising support—and then once in the House have let the matter severely alone——

LORD J. (*to* STONOR). Let it alone! Bless my soul, I should think so indeed.

STONOR. Of course. Only it's a device that's somewhat worn.

(*Enter* MISS LEVERING, *with hat on; gloves and veil in her hand.*)

LORD J. Still if they think they're getting a future Cabinet Minister on their side——

STONOR . . . it will be sufficiently embarrassing for the Cabinet Minister.

(STONOR *turns to speak to* JEAN. *Stops dead seeing* MISS LEVERING.)

JEAN (*smiling*). You know one another?

MISS L. (*looking at* STONOR *with intentness but quite calmly*). Everybody in this part of the world knows Mr. Stonor, but he doesn't know me.

LORD J. Miss Levering.

(*They bow.*)

(*Enter* GREATOREX, *sidling in with an air of giving* MRS. FREDDY *a wide berth.*)

JEAN (*to* MISS LEVERING *with artless enthusiasm*). Oh, have you been hearing him speak?

MISS L. Yes, I was visiting some relations near Dutfield. They took me to hear you.

STONOR. Oh—the night the Suffragettes made their customary row.

MISS L. The night they asked you——

STONOR (*flying at the first chance of distraction, shakes hands with* MRS. FREDDY). Well, Mrs. Freddy, what do you think of your friends now?

MRS. F. My friends?

STONOR (*offering her the Sunday paper*). Yes, the disorderly women.

MRS. F. (*with dignity*). They are not my friends, but I don't think you must call them——

STONOR. Why not? (*Laughs.*) I can forgive them for worrying the late Government. But they *are* disorderly.

MISS L. (*quietly*). Isn't the phrase consecrated to a different class?

GREAT. (*who has got hold of the Sunday paper*). He's perfectly right. How do you do? Disorderly women! That's what they are!

FARN. (*reading over his shoulder*). Ought to be locked up! every one of 'em.

GREAT. (*assenting angrily*). Public nuisances! Going about with dog whips and spitting in policemen's faces.

MRS. F. (*with a harassed air*). I wonder if they did spit?

GREAT. (*exulting*). Of *course* they did.

MRS. F. (*turns on him*). You're no authority on what they do. *You* run away.

GREAT. (*trying to turn the laugh*). Run away? Yes. (*Backing a few paces.*) And if ever I muster up courage to come back, it will be to vote for better manners in public life, not worse than we have already.

MRS. F. (*meekly*). So should I. Don't think that *I* defend the Suffragette methods.

JEAN. (*with cheerful curiosity*). Still, you *are* an advocate of the Suffrage, aren't you?

MRS. F. *Here?* (*Shrugs.*) I don't beat the air.

GREAT. (*mocking*). Only policemen.

MRS. F. (*plaintively*). If you cared to know the attitude of the real workers in the reform, you might have noticed in any paper last week we lost no time in dissociating ourselves from the little group of hysterical—— (*Catches her husband's eye, and instantly checks her flow of words.*)

MRS. H. They have lowered the whole sex in the eyes of the entire world.

JEAN (*joining* GEOFFREY STONOR). I can't quite see what they want—those Suffragettes.

GREAT. Notoriety.

FARN. What they want? A good thrashin'—that's what I'd give 'em.

MISS L. (*murmurs*). Spirited fellow!

LORD J. Well, there's one sure thing—they've dished their goose.

(GREATOREX *chuckles, still reading the account.*)

I believe these silly scenes are a pure joy to you.

GREAT. Final death-blow to the whole silly business!

JEAN (*mystified, looking from one to the other*). The Suffragettes don't seem to *know* they're dead.

GREAT. They still keep up a sort of death-rattle. But they've done for themselves.

JEAN (*clasping her hands with fervour*). Oh, I hope they'll last till the election's over.

FARN. (*stares*). Why?

JEAN. Oh, we want them to get the working man to—(*stumbling and a little confused*)—to vote for . . . the Conservative candidate. Isn't that so?

(*Looking round for help. General laughter.*)

LORD J. Fancy, Jean——!

GREAT. The working man's a good deal of an ass, but even he won't listen to——

JEAN (*again appealing to the silent* STONOR). But he *does* listen like anything! I asked why there were so few at the Long Mitcham meeting, and I was told, "Oh, they've all gone to hear Miss——"

STONOR. Just for a lark, that was.

LORD J. It has no real effect on the vote.

GREAT. Not the smallest.

JEAN (*wide-eyed, to* STONOR). Why, I thought you said——

STONOR (*hastily, rubbing his hand over the lower part of his face and speaking quickly*). I've a notion a little soap and water wouldn't do me any harm.

LORD J. I'll take you up. You know Freddy Tunbridge.

(STONOR *pauses to shake hands. Exeunt all three.*)

JEAN (*perplexed, as* STONOR *turns away, says to* GREATOREX). Well, if women are of no importance in politics, it isn't for the reason you gave. There is now and then a week-ender among them.

GREAT. (*shuffles about uneasily*). Hm—Hm. (*Finds himself near* MRS. FREDDY.) Lord! The perils that beset the feet of man!

(*With an air of comic caution, moves away,* L.)

JEAN (*to* FARNBOROUGH, *aside, laughing*). Why does he behave like that?

FARN. His moral sense is shocked.

JEAN. Why, I saw him and Mrs. Freddy together at the French Play the other night—as thick as thieves.

MISS L. Ah, that was before he knew her revolting views.

JEAN. What revolting views?

GREAT. Sh! Sunday.

(*As* GREATOREX *sidles cautiously further away.*)

JEAN (*laughing in spite of herself*). I can't believe women are so helpless when I see men so afraid of them.

GREAT. The great mistake was in teaching them to read and write.

JEAN (*over* MISS LEVERING'S *shoulder, whispers*). *Say* something.

MISS L. (*to* GREATOREX, *smiling*). Oh no, that wasn't the worst mistake.

GREAT. Yes, it was.

Miss L. No. Believe me. The mistake was *in* letting women learn to talk.

Great. *Ah!* (*Wheels about with sudden rapture.*) I see now what's to be the next great reform.

Miss L. (*holding up the little volume*). When women are all dumb, no more discussions of the "Paradiso."

Great. (*with a gesture of mock rapture*). The thing itself! (*Aside.*) That's a great deal better than talking about it, as I'm sure *you* know.

Miss L. Why do you think I know?

Great. Only the plain women are in any doubt.

(Jean *joins* Miss Levering.)

Great. Wait for me, Farnborough. I cannot go about unprotected.

[*Exeunt* Farnborough *and* Greatorex.

Mrs. F. It's true what that old cynic says. The scene in the House has put back the reform a generation.

Jean. I wish 'd been there.

Mrs. F. I *was*.

Jean. Oh, was it like the papers said?

Mrs. F. Worse. I've never been so moved in public. No tragedy, no great opera ever gripped an audience as the situation in the House did that night. There we all sat breathless—with everything more favourable to us than it had been within the memory of women. Another five minutes and the Resolution would have passed. Then . . . all in a moment——

Lady John (*to* Mrs. Heriot). Listen—they're talking about the female hooligans.

Mrs. H. No, thank you! (*Sits apart with the "Church Times."*)

MRS. F. (*excitedly*). All in a moment a horrible dingy little flag was poked through the gr*i*lle of the Woman's Gallery — cries — insults — scuffling — the police—the *i*gnominious turning out of the women—*us* as well as the—— Oh, I can't *think* of it w*i*thout——

(*Jumps up and walks to and fro.*)

(*Pauses.*) Then the next morning! The people gloating. Our friends antagonised—people who were wavering—nearly won over—all thrown back—heart breaking! Even my husband! Freddy's been an angel about letting me take my share when I felt I must—but of course I've always known he doesn't really like it. It makes him shy. I'm sure it gives him a horr*i*d twist inside when he sees my name among the speakers on the placards. But he's always been an angel about it before th*i*s. After the d*i*sgraceful scene he said, "It just shows how unfit women are for any sort of coherent th*i*nking or concerted action."

JEAN. To think that it should be women who've g*i*ven the Cause the worst blow it ever had!

Mrs. F. The work of forty years destroyed in five minutes!

JEAN. They must have felt pretty s*i*ck when they woke up the next morning—the Suffragettes.

MRS. F. I don't waste any sympathy on *them*. I'm thinking of the penalty *all* women have to pay because a handful of hysterical——

JEAN. Still I think I'm sorry for them. It must be dreadful to find you've done such a lot of harm to the thing you care most about in the world.

MISS L. Do you picture the Suffragettes s*i*tting in sackcloth ?

MRS. F. Well, they can't help realising *now* what they've done.

MISS L. (*quietly*). Isn't it just possible they realise they've waked up interest in the Woman Question so that it's advertised in every paper and discussed in every house from Land's End to John o'Groats? Don't you think *they* know there's been more said and written about it in these ten days since the scene, than in the ten years before it?

MRS. F. You aren't saying you think it was a good way to get what they wanted?

MISS L. (*shrugs*). I'm only pointing out that it seems not such a bad way to get it known they *do* want something—and (*smiling*) "want it bad."

JEAN (*getting up*). Didn't Mr. Greatorex say women had been politely petitioning Parliament for forty years?

MISS L. And men have only laughed.

JEAN. But they'd come round. (*She looks from one to the other.*) Mrs. Tunbridge says, before that horrid scene, everything was favourable at last

MISS L. At last? Hadn't it been just as "favourable" before?

MRS. F. No. We'd never had so many members pledged to our side.

MISS L. I thought I'd heard somebody say the Bill had got as far as that, time and time again.

JEAN. Oh no. Surely not——

MRS. F. (*reluctantly*). Y-yes. This was only a Resolution. The Bill passed a second reading thirty-seven years ago.

JEAN (*with wide eyes*). And what difference did it make?

MISS L. The men laughed rather louder.

MRS. F. Oh, it's got as far as a second reading several times—but we never had so many *friends* in the House before——

MISS L. (*with a faint smile*). "Friends!"

JEAN. Why do you say it like that?

MISS L. Perhaps because I was think*ing* of a funny story—he said it was funny—a Liberal Wh*ip* told me the other day. A Radical Member went out of the House after his speech in favour of the Woman's Bill, and as he came back half an hour later, he heard some Members talking in the Lobby about the astonishing number who were going to vote for the measure. And the Fr*ie*nd of Woman dropped his jaw and clutched the man next him: "My God!" he said, "you don't mean to say they're go*in*g to give it to them!"

JEAN. Oh!

MRS. F. You don't th*in*k all men in Parl*ia*ment are l*i*ke that!

MISS L. I don't th*in*k all men are burglars, but I lock my doors.

JEAN (*below her breath*). You th*in*k that night of the scene—you think the men didn't *mean* to play fa*i*r?

MISS L. (*her coolness in contrast to the excitement of the others*). Didn't the women sit quiet till ten minutes to closing time?

JEAN. Ten m*i*nutes to settle a quest*i*on like that!

MISS L. (*quietly to* MRS. FREDDY). Couldn't you see the men were at their old game?

LADY JOHN (*coming forward*). You th*in*k they were just putting off the issue till it was too late?

MISS L. (*in a detached tone*). *I* wasn't there, but I haven't heard anybody deny that the women wa*i*ted till ten minutes to eleven. Then they d*i*scovered the policeman who'd been sent up at the psychological moment to the back of the gallery. Then, I'm told, when the women saw they were betrayed once more, they utilised the few minutes left, to impress on the country at large the fact of their demands—did it in the only way left them.

(*Sits leaning forward reflectively smiling, chin in hand.*)

It does rather look to the outsider as if the well-behaved women had worked for forty years and made less impression on the world then those fiery young women made in five minutes.

MRS. F. Oh, come, be fair!

MISS L. Well, you must admit that, next day, every newspaper reader in Europe and America knew there were women in England in such dead earnest about the Suffrage that the men had stopped laughing at last, and turned them out of the House. Men even advertised how little they appreciated the fun by sending the women to gaol in pretty sober earnest. And all the world was talking about it.

(MRS. HERIOT *lays down the "Church Times" and joins the others.*)

LADY JOHN. I have noticed, whenever the men aren't there, the women sit and discuss that scene.

JEAN (*cheerfully*). *I* shan't have to wait till the men are gone. (*Leans over* LADY JOHN'S *shoulder and says half aside*) He's in sympathy.

LADY JOHN. How do you know?

JEAN. He told the interrupting women so.

(MRS. FREDDY *looks mystified. The others smile.*)

LADY JOHN. Oh!

(MR. FREDDY *and* LORD JOHN *appear by the door they went out of. They stop to talk.*)

MRS. F. Here's Freddy! (*Lower, hastily to* MISS LEVERING.) You're judging from the outside. Those of us who have been working for years . . . we all realise it was a perfectiy lunatic proceeding. Why, *think!* The only chance of our getting what we want is by *winning over* the men.

(*Her watchful eye, leaving her husband for a moment, catches* MISS LEVERING'S *little involuntary gesture.*)

What's the matter?

MISS L. "Winning over the men" has been the woman's way for centuries. Do you think the result should make us proud of our policy? Yes? Then go and walk in Piccadilly at midnight.

(*The older women glance at* JEAN.)

No, I forgot——

MRS. H. (*with majesty*). Yes, it's not the first time you've forgotten.

MISS L. I forgot the magistrate's ruling. He said no decent woman had any business to be in London's main thoroughfare at night unless she has *a man with her*. I heard that in Nine Elms, too. "You're obliged to take up with a chap!" was what the woman said.

MRS. H. (*rising*). JEAN! Come!

(*She takes* JEAN *by her arm and draws her to the window, where she signals* GREATOREX *and* FARNBOROUGH. MRS. FREDDY *joins her husband and* LORD JOHN.)

LADY JOHN (*kindly, aside to* MISS LEVERING). My dear, I th*i*nk Lydia Heriot's r*i*ght. We oughtn't to do anything or *say* anything to encourage this ferment of feminism, and I'll tell you why : it's l*i*kely to bring a very terr*i*ble thing in its train.

MISS L. What terr*i*ble th*i*ng?

LADY JOHN. Sex antagonism.

MISS L. (*rising*). It's here.

LADY JOHN (*very gravely*). Don't say that.

(JEAN *has quietly disengaged herself from* MRS. HERIOT, *and the group at the window returns and stands behind* LADY JOHN, *looking up into* MISS LEVERING'S *face.*)

MISS L. (*to* LADY JOHN). You're so conscious it's here, you're afraid to have it mentioned.

LADY JOHN (*turning and seeing* JEAN. *Rising hastily*). If it's here, it is the fault of those women agitators.

MISS L. (*gently*). No woman *begins* that way. (*Leans forward with clasped hands looking into vacancy.*) Every woman's in a state of natural subjection (*smiles at* JEAN)—no, I'd rather say allegiance to her *i*dea of romance and her hope of motherhood. They're embod*i*ed for her in man. They're the strongest things in l*i*fe—t*i*ll man kills them.

(*Rousing herself and looking into* LADY JOHN'S *face.*)

Let's be fair. Each woman knows why that alleg*i*ance d*i*ed.

(LADY JOHN *turns hastily, sees* LORD JOHN *coming down with* MR. FREDDY *and meets them at the foot of the stairs.* MISS LEVERING *has turned to the table looking for her gloves, &c., among the papers; unconsciously drops the handkerchief she had in her little book.)*

JEAN (*in a low voice to* MISS LEVERING). All this talk against the wicked Suffragettes—it makes me want to go and hear what they've got to say for themselves.

MISS L. (*smiling with a non-committal air as she finds the veil she's been searching for*). Well, they're holding a meeting in Trafalgar Square at three o'clock.

JEAN. This afternoon? But that's no use to people out of town—— Unless I could invent some excuse .

LORD J. (*benevolently*). Still talking over the Shelter plans?

MISS L. No. We left the Shelter some time ago.

LORD J. (*to* JEAN). Then what's all the chatterment about?

(JEAN, *a little confused, looks at* MISS LEVERING.)

MISS L. The latest thing in veils. (*Ties hers round her hat.*)

GREAT. The invincible frivolity of woman!

LORD J. (*genially*). Don't scold them. It's a very proper topic.

MISS L. (*whimsically*). Oh, I was afraid you'd despise us for it.

BOTH MEN (*with condescension*). Not at all—not at all.

JEAN (*to* MISS LEVERING *as* FOOTMAN *appears*). Oh, they're coming for you. Don't forget your book.

(FOOTMAN *holds out a salver with a telegram on it for* JEAN.)

Why, it's for me!

MISS L. But it's time I was——

(*Crosses to table.*)

JEAN (*opening the telegram*). May I? (*Reads, and glances over the paper at* MISS LEVERING.) I've got your book. (*Crosses to* MISS LEVERING, *and, looking at the back of the volume*) Dante! Whereabouts are you? (*Opening at the marker.*) Oh, the "Inferno."

MISS L. No; I'm in a worse place.

JEAN. I didn't know there was a worse.

MISS L. Yes; it's worse with the Vigliacchi.

JEAN. I forget. Were they Guelf or Ghibelline?

MISS L. (*smiling*). They weren't either, and that was why Dante couldn't stand them. (*More gravely.*) He said there was no place in Heaven nor in Purgatory—not even a corner in Hell—for the souls who had stood aloof from strife. (*Looking steadily into the girl's eyes.*) He called them "wretches who never lived," Dante did, because they'd never felt the pangs of partizanship. And so they wander homeless on the skirts of limbo among the abortions and off-scourings of Creation.

JEAN (*a long breath after a long look. When* MISS LEVERING *has turned away to make her leisurely adieux* JEAN'S *eyes fall on the open telegram*). Aunt Ellen, I've got to go to London.

(STONOR, *re-entering, hears this, but pretends to talk to* MR. FREDDY, *&c.*)

LADY JOHN. My dear child!

MRS. H. Nonsense! Is your grandfather worse?

JEAN (*folding the telegram*). No-o. I don't think so. But it's necessary I should go, all the same.

MRS. H. Go away when Mr. Stonor——

JEAN. He said he'd have to leave directly after luncheon.

LADY JOHN. I'll just see Miss Levering off, and then I'll come back and talk about it.

LORD J. (*to* MISS LEVERING). Why are you saying goodbye as if you were never coming back?

MISS L. (*smiling*). One never knows. Maybe I shan't come back. (*To* STONOR.) Goodbye.

(STONOR *bows ceremoniously. The others go up laughing.* STONOR *comes down.*)

JEAN (*impulsively*). There mayn't be another train! Miss Levering——

STONOR (*standing in front of her*). What if there isn't? I'll take you back in the motor.

JEAN (*rapturously*). *Will* you? (*Inadvertently drops the telegram.*) I must be there by three!

STONOR (*picks up the telegram and a handkerchief lying near, glances at the message*). Why, it's only an invitation to dine—Wednesday!

JEAN. Sh! (*Takes the telegram and puts it in her pocket.*)

STONOR. Oh, I see! (*Lower, smiling.*) It's rather dear of you to arrange our going off like that. You *are* a clever little girl!

JEAN. It's not that I was arranging. I want to hear those women in Trafalgar Square—the Suffragettes.

STONOR (*incredulous, but smiling*). How perfectly absurd! (*Looking after* LADY JOHN.) Besides, I expect she wouldn't like my carrying you off like that.

JEAN. Then she'll have to make an excuse and come too.

STONOR. Ah, it wouldn't be qu*i*te the same——

JEAN (*rapidly thinking it out*). We could get back here *i*n t*i*me for dinner.

(GEOFFREY STONOR *glances down at the handkerchief still in his hand, and turns it half mechanically from corner to corner.*)

JEAN (*absent-mindedly*). Mine?

STONOR (*hastily, without reflection*). No. (*Hands it to* MISS LEVERING *as she passes.*) Yours.

(MISS LEVERING, *on her way to the lobby with* LORD JOHN *seems not to notice.*)

JEAN (*takes the handkerchief to give to her, glancing down at the embroidered corner; stops*). But that's not an L! It's Vi——!

(GEOFFREY STONOR *suddenly turns his back and takes up the newspaper.*)

LADY JOHN (*from the lobby*). Come, V*i*da, s*i*nce you will go.

MISS L. Yes; I'm com*i*ng.

[*Exit* MISS LEVERING.

JEAN. *I* didn't know her name was Vida; how did you?

(STONOR *stares silently over the top of his paper.*)

CURTAIN.

ACT II

SCENE: *The north side of the Nelson Column in Trafalgar Square. The Curtain rises on an uproar. The crowd, which momentarily increases, is composed chiefly of weedy youths and wastrel old men. There are a few decent artisans; three or four "beery" out-o'-works; three or four young women of the domestic servant or Strand restaurant cashier class; one aged woman in rusty black peering with faded, wondering eyes, consulting the faces of the men and laughing nervously and apologetically from time to time; one or two quiet-looking, business-like women, thirty to forty; two middle-class men, who stare and whisper and smile. A quiet old man with a lot of unsold Sunday papers under one arm stands in an attitude of rapt attention, with the free hand round his deaf ear. A brisk-looking woman of forty-five or so, wearing pince-nez, goes round with a pile of propagandist literature on her arm. Many of the men smoking cigarettes—the old ones pipes. On the outskirts of this crowd, of several hundred, a couple of smart men in tall shining hats hover a few moments, single eyeglass up, and then saunter off. Against the middle of the Column, where it rises above the stone platform, is a great red banner, one supporting pole upheld by a grimy sandwichman, the other by a small, dirty boy of eight. If practicable only the lower portion of the banner need be seen, bearing the final words of the legend—*

"VOTES FOR WOMEN!"

in immense white letters. It will be well to get, to the full, the effect of the height above the crowd of the straggling group of speakers on the pedestal platform. These are, as the Curtain rises, a working-class woman who is waving her arms and talking very earnestly, her voice for the moment blurred in the uproar. She is dressed in brown serge and looks pinched and sallow. At her side is the CHAIRMAN *urging that she be given a fair hearing.* ALLEN TRENT *is a tall, slim, brown-haired man of twenty-eight, with a slight stoop, an agreeable aspect, well-bred voice, and the gleaming brown eye of the visionary. Behind these two, looking on or talking among themselves, are several other carelessly dressed women; one, better turned out than the rest, is quite young, very slight and gracefully built, with round, very pink cheeks, full, scarlet lips, naturally waving brown hair, and an air of childish gravity. She looks at the unruly mob with imperturbable calm. The* CHAIRMAN'S *voice is drowned.)*

WORKING WOMAN (*with lean, brown finger out and voice raised shriller now above the tumult*). I've got boys o' me own and we laugh at all sorts o' things, but I should be ashymed and so would they if ever they was to be'yve as you're doin' to-d'y.

(*In laughter the noise dies.*)

People 'ave been sayin' this is a middle-class woman's movement. It's a libel. I'm a workin' woman myself, the wife of a working man. (*Voice:* "Pore devil!") I'm a Poor Law Guardian and a——

NOISY YOUNG MAN. Think of that, now—gracious me!

(*Laughter and interruption.*)

OLD NEWSVENDOR (*to the noisy young man near him*). Oh, shut up, cawn't yer?

NOISY YOUNG MAN. Not fur *you!*

VOICE. Go 'ome and darn yer old man's stockens!

VOICE. Just clean yer *own* doorstep!

WORKING WOMAN. It's a pore sort of 'ousekeeper that leaves 'er doorstep till Sunday afternoon. Maybe that's when you would do *your* doorstep. I do mine in the mornin' before you men are awake.

OLD NEWSVENDOR. It's true, wot she says!—every word.

WORKING WOMAN. You say we women 'ave got no business servin' on boards and thinkin' about politics. Wot's *politics?*

(*A derisive roar.*)

It's just 'ousekeepin' on a big scyle. 'Oo among you workin' men 'as the most comfortable 'omes? Those of you that gives yer wives yer wyges.

(*Loud laughter and jeers.*)

VOICES. { That's it!
Wantin' our money.
Lord 'Igh 'Ousekeeper of England.

WORKING WOMAN. If it wus only to use fur *our* comfort, d'ye think many o' you workin' men would be found turnin' over their wyges to their *wives*? No! Wot's the reason thousands do—and the best and the soberest? Because the work*in*' man knows that wot's a pound to *'im* is twenty shillin's to 'is wife. And she'll myke every penny in every one o' them shillin's *tell*. She gets more fur *'im* out of 'is wyges than wot 'e can! Some o' you know wot the 'omes is l*i*ke w'ere the men don't let the women manage. Well, the Poor Laws and the 'ole Government is just in the syme muddle because the men 'ave tr*i*ed to do the national 'ousekeepin' without the women.

(*Roars.*)

But, l*i*ke I told you before, it's a l*i*bel to say it's only the well-off women wot's wantin' the vote. Wot about the 96,000 textile workers? Wot about the Yorksh*i*re tailoresses? I can tell you wot plenty o' the poor women think about it. I'm one of them, and I can tell you we see there's reforms needed. *We ought to 'ave the vote* (*jeers*), and we know 'ow to appreciate the other women 'oo go to pr*i*son fur tryin' to get it fur us!

(*With a little final bob of emphasis and a glance over shoulder at the old woman and the young one behind her, she seems about to retire, but pauses as the murmur in the crowd grows into distinct phrases.* "They get their 'air cut free." "Naow they don't, that's only us!" "Silly Suffragettes!" "Stop at 'ome!" "'Inderin' policemen—mykin' rows in the streets!")

VOICE (*louder than the others*). They sees yer a*i*n't fit t'ave——

OTHER VOICES. "Ha, ha!" "Shut up!" "Keep quiet, cawn't yer?" (*General uproar.*)

CHAIRMAN. You evidently don't know what had to be done by *men* before the extension of the Suffrage in '67. If it hadn't been for demonstrations of violence——

(*His voice is drowned.*)

WORKING WOMAN (*coming forward again, her shrill note rising clear*). You s'y woman's plyce is 'ome! Don't you know there's a third of the women o' this country can't afford the luxury of stayin' in their 'omes? They *got* to go out and 'elp make money to p'y the rent and keep the 'ome from bein' sold up. Then there's all the women that 'aven't got even miseerable 'omes. They 'aven't got any 'omes *at all.*

NOISY YOUNG MAN. You said *you* got one. W'y don't you stop in it?

WORKING WOMAN. Yes, that's like a man. If one o' you is all right, he thinks the rest don't matter. We women——

NOISY YOUNG MAN. The lydies! God bless 'em!

(*Voices drown her and the* CHAIRMAN.)

OLD NEWSVENDOR (*to* NOISY YOUNG MAN). Oh, take that extra 'alf pint 'ome and *sleep it off!*

WORKING WOMAN. P'r'aps *your* 'omes are all right. P'r'aps you aren't livin', old and young, married and single, in one room. I come from a plyce where many fam'lies 'ave to live like that if they're to go on livin' *at all.* If you don't believe me, come and let me show you! (*She spreads out her lean arms.*) Come with me to Canning Town!—come with me to Bromley—come to Poplar and to Bow! No. You won't even *think* about the overworked women and the underfed children and the 'ovels they *live* in. And you want that we shouldn't think *neither*——

A VAGRANT. We'll do the thinkin'. You go 'ome and nuss the byby.

WORKING WOMAN. I do nurse my byby! I've nursed seven. What 'ave you done for yours? P'r'aps your children never goes 'ungry, and maybe you're satisfied—though I must say I wouldn't a' thought it from the *look* o' you.

VOICE. Oh, I s'y!

WORKING WOMAN. But we women are not satisfied. We don't only want better *things* for our own children. We want better *things* for all. *Every* child is our child. We know in our 'earts we oughtn't to rest till we've mothered 'em every one.

VOICE. "Women"—"*children*"—wot about the *men?* Are *they* all 'appy?

(*Derisive laughter and* "No! no!" "Not precisely." "'Appy? Lord!")

WORKING WOMAN. No, there's lots o' you men I'm sorry for (*Shrill Voice:* "Thanks awfully!"), an' we'll 'elp you *if* you let us.

VOICE. 'Elp us? You tyke the bread out of our mouths. You women are black-leggin' the men!

WORKING WOMAN. *W'y* does any woman tyke less wyges than a man for the same work? Only because we can't get anything better. That's part the reason w'y we're yere to-d'y. Do you reely *think* we tyke them there low wyges because we got a *lykin'* for low wyges? No. We're just like you. We want as much as ever we can get. ("'Ear! 'Ear!" *and laughter.*) We got a gryte deal to do with our wyges, we women has. We got the *children* to think about. And w'en we get our rights, a woman's flesh and blood won't be so much cheaper than a man's that employers can get rich on keepin' you out o' work, and sweatin' us. If you men only could see it, we got the *syme* cause, and if you 'elped us you'd be 'elpin yerselves.

VOICES. "Rot!" "Drivel."

OLD NEWSVENDOR. True as gospel!

(*She retires against the banner with the others. There is some applause.*)

A MAN (*patronisingly*). Well, now, that wusn't so bad—fur a woman.

ANOTHER. N-naw. *Not fur a woman.*

CHAIRMAN (*speaking through this last*). Miss Ernestine Blunt will now address you.

(*Applause, chiefly ironic, laughter, a general moving closer and knitting up of attention.* ERNESTINE BLUNT *is about twenty-four, but looks younger. She is very downright, not to say pugnacious—the something amusing and attractive about her is there, as it were, against her will, and the more fetching for that. She has no conventional gestures, and none of any sort at first. As she warms to her work she uses her slim hands to enforce her emphasis, but as though unconsciously. Her manner of speech is less monotonous than that of the average woman-speaker, but she, too, has a fashion of leaning all her weight on the end of the sentence. She brings out the final word or two with an effort of underscoring, and makes a forward motion of the slim body as if the better to drive the last nail in.*

She evidently means to be immensely practical—the kind who is pleased to think she hasn't a grain of sentimentality in her composition, and whose feeling, when it does all but master her, communicates itself magnetically to others.)

MISS ERNESTINE BLUNT. Perhaps I'd better begin by explaining a little about our "tactics."

(*Cries of* "Tactics! We know!" "Mykin' trouble!" "Public scandal!")

To make you understand what we've done, I must remind you of what others have done. Perhaps you don't know that women first petitioned Parliament for the Franchise as long ago as 1866.

VOICE. How do *you* know?

(*She pauses a moment, taken off her guard by the suddenness of the attack.*)

VOICE. You wasn't there!

VOICE. That was the trouble. Haw! haw!

MISS E. B. And the petition was presented——

VOICE. Give 'er a 'earin' now she 'as got out of 'er crydle.

MISS E. B. —presented to the House of Commons by that great Liberal, John Stuart Mill. (*Voice:* "Mill? Who is he when he's at home?") Bills or Resolutions have been before the House on and off for the last thirty-six years. That, roughly, is our history. We found ourselves, towards the close of the year 1905, with no assurance that if we went on in the same way any girl born into the world in this generation would live to exercise the rights of citizenship, though she lived to be a hundred. So we said all this has been *in* vain. We must try some other way. How did the working man get the Suffrage, we asked ourselves? Well, we turned up the records, and we *saw*——

VOICES. "Not by scratching people's faces!" "Disraeli give it 'em!" "Dizzy? Get out!" "Cahnty Cahncil scholarships!" "Oh, Lord, this education!" "Chartist riots, she's thinkin' of!" (*Noise in the crowd.*)

MISS E. B. But we don't *want* to follow such a violent example. We would much rather *not*—but *if* that's the only way we can make the country see we're in earnest, we are prepared to show them.

VOICE. An' they'll show you!—Give you another month 'ard.

MISS E. B. Don't think that going to prison has any fears for us. We'd go *for life* if by doing that we could get freedom for the rest of the women.

VOICES. "Hear, hear!" "Rot!" "W'y don't the men 'elp ye to get your rights?"

MISS E. B. Here's some one asking why the men don't help. It's partly they don't understand yet—they *will* before we've done! (*Laughter.*) Partly they don't understand yet what's at stake——

RESPECTABLE OLD MAN (*chuckling*). Lord, they're a 'educatin' of us!

VOICE. Wot next?

MISS E. B. —and partly that the bravest man is afraid of ridicule. Oh, yes; we've heard a great deal all our lives about the timidity and the sensitiveness of women. And it's true. We *are* sensitive. But I tell you, ridicule crumples a man up. It steels a woman. We've come to know the value of ridicule. We've educated ourselves so that we welcome ridicule. We owe our sincerest thanks to the comic writers.

The cartoon*i*st is our unconsc*i*ous fr*i*end. Who cartoons people who are of no importance? What advertisement is so sure of being remembered?

POETIC YOUNG MAN. I adm*i*t that.

MISS E. B. If we didn't know it by any other sign, the comic papers would tell us *we've arrived!* But our greatest debt of grat*i*tude we owe, to the man who called us female hooligans.

(*The crowd bursts into laughter.*)

We aren't hooligans, but we hope the fact will be overlooked. If everybody said we were nice, well-behaved women, who'd come to hear us? *Not the men.*

(*Roars.*)

Men tell us it *i*sn't womanly for us to care about politics. How do they know what's womanly? It's for women to dec*i*de that. Let the men attend to being manly. It will take them all their t*i*me.

VOICE. Are we down-'earted? Oh no!

MISS E. B. And they say it would be dreadful *i*f we got the vote, because then we'd be pitted against men in the economic struggle. But that's come about already. Do you know that out of every hundred women in this country eighty-two are wage-earning women? It used to be thought unfeminine for women to be students and to aspire to the arts—that bring fame and fortune. But nobody has ever sa*i*d it was unfeminine for women to do the heavy drudgery that's badly paid. That kind of work had to be done by *some*body—and the men didn't hanker after it. Oh, no.

(*Laughter and interruption.*)

A MAN ON THE OUTER FRINGE. She can *talk*—the little one can.

ANOTHER. Oh, they can all "talk."

A BEERY, DIRTY FELLOW OF FIFTY. I wouldn't like to be 'er 'usban' Think o' comin' 'ome to *that!*

HIS PAL. I'd soon learn 'er!

MISS E. B. (*speaking through the noise*). Oh, no! *Let* the women scrub and cook and wash. That's all right! But if they want to try their hand at the better paid work of the *li*beral professions—oh, very unfeminine indeed! Then there's another thing. Now I want you to listen to this, because it's *very* important. Men say if we persist in competing with them for the bigger prizes, they're dreadfully afraid we'd lose the beautiful protecting chivalry that—— Yes, I don't wonder you laugh. *We* laugh. (*Bending forward with lit eyes.*) But the women I found at the Ferry Tin Works working for five shillings a week —I didn't see them laughing. The beautiful ch*i*valry of the employers of women doesn't prevent them from paying women tenpence a day for sorting coal and loading and unloading carts—doesn't prevent them from forcing women to earn bread in ways worse still. So we won't talk about chivalry. It's being over-sarcastic. We'll just let this poor ghost of chivalry go—in exchange for a little pla*i*n justice.

VOICE. If the House of Commons won't give you justice, why don't you go to the House of Lords?

MISS E. B. What?

VOICE. Better 'urry up. Case of early clos*i*n'.

(*Laughter. A man at the back asks the speaker something.*)

MISS E. B. (*unable to hear*). You'll be allowed to ask any question you like at the end of the meeting.

NEW-COMER (*boy of eighteen*). Oh, is it question time? I s'y, Miss, 'oo killed cock robin?

(*She is about to resume, but above the general noise the voice of a man at the back reaches her indistinct but insistent. She leans forward trying to catch what he says. While the indistinguishable murmur has been going on* GEOFFREY STONOR *has appeared on the edge of the crowd, followed by* JEAN *and* LADY JOHN *in motor veils.*)

JEAN (*pressing forward eagerly and raising her veil*). Is she one of them? That little thing!

STONOR (*doubtfully*). I—I suppose so.

JEAN. Oh, ask some one, Geoffrey. I'm so disappointed. I did so hope we'd hear one of the—the worst.

MISS E. B. (*to the interrupter—on the other side*). What? What do you say? (*She screws up her eyes with the effort to hear, and puts a hand up to her ear. A few indistinguishable words between her and the man.*)

LADY JOHN (*who has been studying the figures on the platform through her lorgnon, turns to a working man beside her*). Can you tell me, my man, which are the ones that—a—that make the disturbances?

WORKING MAN. The one that's doing the talking—she's the disturbingest o' the lot.

JEAN (*craning to listen*). Not that nice little——

WORKING MAN. Don't you be took in, Miss.

MISS E. B. Oh, yes—I see. There's a man over here asking——

A YOUNG MAN. *I've* got a question, too. Are—you—married?

ANOTHER (*sniggering*). Quick! There's yer chawnce. 'E's a bachelor.

(*Laughter.*)

MISS E. B. (*goes straight on as if she had not heard*) —man asking: if the women get full citizenship, and a war is declared, will the women fight?

POETIC YOUNG MAN. No, really—no, really, now!

(*The Crowd:* "Haw! Haw!" "Yes!" "Yes, how about *that?*")

MISS E. B. (*smiling*). Well, you know, some people say the whole trouble about us is that we *do* fight. But it is only hard necessity makes us do that. We don't *want* to fight—as men seem to—just for fighting's sake. Women are for peace.

VOICE. Hear, hear.

MISS E. B. And when we have a share in public affairs there'll be less likelihood of war. But that's not to say women can't fight. The Boer women did. The Russian women face conflicts worse than any battlefield can show. (*Her voice shakes a little, and the eyes fill, but she controls her emotion gallantly, and dashes on.*) But we women know all that is evil, and we're for peace. Our part—we're proud to remember it—our part has been to go about after you men in war-time, and—*pick up the pieces!*

(*A great shout.*)

Yes—seems funny, doesn't it? You men blow them to bits, and then we come along and put them together again. If you know anything about military nursing, you know a good deal of our work has been done in the face of danger—*but it's always been done.*

OLD NEWSVENDOR. That's so. That's so.

MISS E. B. You complain that more and more we're taking away from you men the work that's always been yours. You can't any longer keep women out of the industries. The only question is upon what terms shall she continue to be in? As long as she's in on bad terms, she's not only hurting herself—she's hurting you. But if you're feeling discouraged about our competing with you, we're willing to leave you your trade in war. *Let* the men take life! We *give* life! (*Her voice is once more moved and proud.*) No one will pretend ours isn't one of the dangerous trades either. I won't say any more to you now, because we've got others to speak to you, and a new woman-helper that I want you to hear.

(*She retires to the sound of clapping. There's a hurried consultation between her and the* CHAIRMAN. *Voices in the Crowd:* "The little 'un's all right" "Ernestine's a corker," &c.)

JEAN (*looking at* STONOR *to see how he's taken it*). Well?

STONOR (*smiling down at her*). Well——

JEAN. Nothing reprehensible in what *she* said, was there?

STONOR (*shrugs*). Oh, reprehensible!

JEAN. It makes me rather miserable all the same.

STONOR (*draws her hand protectingly through his arm*). You mustn't take it as much to heart as all that.

JEAN. I can't help it—I can't indeed, Geoffrey. I shall *never* be able to make a speech like that!

STONOR (*taken aback*). I hope not, indeed.

JEAN. Why, I thought you said you wanted me——?

STONOR (*smiling*). To make nice little speeches with composure—so I did! So I—— (*Seems to lose his thread as he looks at her.*)

JEAN (*with a little frown*). You *said*——

STONOR. That you have very pink cheeks? Well, I stick to that.

JEAN (*smiling*). Sh! Don't tell everybody.

STONOR. And you're the only female creature I ever saw who didn't look a fright in motor things.

JEAN (*melted and smiling*). I'm glad you don't think me a fright.

CHAIRMAN. I will now ask (*name indistinguishable*) to address the meeting.

JEAN (*as she sees* LADY JOHN *moving to one side*). Oh, don't go yet, Aunt Ellen!

LADY JOHN. Go? Certainly not. I want to hear another. (*Craning her neck.*) I can't believe, you know, she was really one of the worst.

(*A big, sallow Cockney has come forward. His scanty hair grows in wisps on a great bony skull.*)

VOICE. That's Pilcher.

ANOTHER. 'Oo's Pilcher?

ANOTHER. If you can't afford a bottle of Tatcho, w'y don't you get yer 'air cut.

MR. P. (*not in the least discomposed*). I've been addressin' a big meetin' at 'Ammersmith this morning, and w'en I told 'em I wus comin' 'ere this awfternoon to speak fur the women—well—then the usual thing began!

(*An appreciative roar from the crowd.*)

In these times if you want peace and quiet at a publ*i*c meetin'——

(*The crowd fills in the hiatus with laughter.*)

There was a man at 'Ammersmith, too, talk*i*n' about women's sphere be*i*n' 'ome. *'Ome* do you call it? You've got a kennel w'ere you can munch your tommy. You've got a corner w'ere you can curl up fur a few hours till you go out to work aga*i*n. No, my man, there's too many of you ain't able to *give* the women 'omes—fit to l*i*ve *i*n, too many of you in that fix fur you to go on jaw*i*n' at those o' the women 'oo want to myke the 'omes a little decenter.

VOICE. If the vote a*i*n't done us any good, 'ow'll it do the women any good?

MR. P. Look 'ere! Any men here belongin' to the Labour Party?

(*Shouts and applause.*)

Well, I don't need to tell these men the vote 'as done us *som*e good. They know it. And it'll do us a lot more good w'en you know 'ow to use the power you got *i*n your 'and.

VOICE. Power! It's those fellers at the bottom o' the street that's got the power.

MR. P. It's you, and men like you, that gave it to 'em. You carried the L*i*berals *i*nto Parliament Street on your own shoulders.

(*Complacent applause.*)

You bel*i*eved all their fine words. You never asked yourselves, "*Wot's a Liberal, anyw'y?*"

A VOICE. He's a jolly good fellow.

(*Cheers and booing.*)

MR. P. No, 'e ain't, or if 'e is jolly, it's only because 'e thinks you're such silly codfish you'll go swellin' his majority again. (*Laughter, in which* STONOR *joins.*) It's enough to make any L*i*beral jolly to see sheep like you lookin' on, proud and 'appy, while you see Liberal leaders desertin' Liberal principles.

(*Voices in agreement and protest.*)

You show me a Liberal, and I'll show you a Mr. Fycing-both-W'ys. Yuss.

(STONOR *moves closer with an amused look.*)

'E sheds the light of 'is warm and 'andsome smile on the working man, and round on the other side 'e's tippin' a wink to the great land-owners. That's to let 'em know 'e's standin' between them and the Soc*i*alists. Huh ! Socialists. Yuss, *Socialists !*

(*General laughter, in which* STONOR *joins.*)

The Liberal, e's the judicial sort o' chap that sits in the middle——

VOICE. On the fence !

MR. P. Tories one side—Soc*i*alists the other. Well it ain't always so comfortable in the middle. You're like to get squeezed. Now, I s'y to the women, the Conservatives don't promise you much but what they promise they *do !*

STONOR (*to* JEAN). This fellow isn't half bad.

MR. P. The Liberals—they'll promise you the earth, and give yer . . . the whole o' noth*i*ng.

(*Roars of approval.*)

JEAN. *Isn't* it fun ? Now, aren't you glad I brought you ?

STONOR (*laughing*). Th*i*s chap's rather amus*i*ng !

MR. P. We men 'ave seen it 'appen over and over. But the women can tyke a 'int quicker'n what we can. They won't stand the nonsense men do. Only they 'aven't got a f*ai*r chawnce even to agitate fur their rights. As I wus comin' up 'ere I 'eard a man sayin', "Look at this big crowd. W'y, we're all *men!* If the women want the vote w'y ain't they 'ere to s'y so?" Well, I'll tell you w'y. It's because they've 'ad to get the d*i*nner fur you and me, and now they're washin' up the d*i*shes.

A VOICE. D'yon think *we* ought to st'y 'ome and wash the dishes?

MR. P. (*laughs good-naturedly*). If they'd leave it to us once or tw*i*ce per'aps we'd understand a little more about the Woman Question. I know w'y *my* wife *i*sn't here. It's because she *knows* I ain't much use round the 'ouse, and she's 'op*i*n' I can talk to some purpose. Maybe she's mistaken. Any'ow, here I am to vote for her and all the other women.

("*Hear! hear!*" "*Oh-h!*")

And to tell you men what *i*mprovements you can expect to see when women 'as the share in publ*i*c affairs they *ought* to 'ave!

VOICE. What do you know about it? You can't even talk grammar.

MR. P. (*is dashed a fraction of a moment, for the first and only time*). I'm not 'ere to talk grammar but to talk Reform. I ain't defendin' my grammar—but I'll say in pawssing that if my mother 'ad 'ad 'er rights, maybe my grammar would have been better.

(STONOR *and* JEAN *exchange smiles. He takes her arm again and bends his head to whisper something in her ear. She listens with lowered eyes and happy face. The discreet love-making goes on during the next few sentences. Interruption. One voice insistent but not clear. The speaker waits only a second and then resumes. "Yes, if the women," but he cannot instantly make himself heard. The boyish* CHAIRMAN *looks harassed and anxious.* MISS ERNESTINE BLUNT *alert, watchful.*)

MR. P. Wait a bit—'arf a m*i*nute, my man!

VOICE. 'Oo yer talk*i*n' to? I ain't your man.

MR. P. Lucky for me! There seems to be a *gentleman* 'ere who doesn't th*i*nk women ought to 'ave the vote.

VOICE. *One?* Oh-h!

(*Laughter.*)

MR. P. Per'aps 'e doesn't know much about women?

(*Indistinguishable repartee.*)

Oh, the gentleman says 'e's married. Well, then, fur the syke of 'is wife we musn't be too sorry 'e's 'ere. No doubt she's s'ying: "'Eaven by prysed those women are mykin' a Demonstrytion in Trafalgar Square, and I'll 'ave a little peace and quiet at 'ome for one Sunday in my life."

(*The crowd laughs and there are jeers for the interrupter—and at the speaker.*)

(*Pointing.*) Why, *you're* like the man at 'Ammersmith this morn*i*ng. 'E was awskin' me: "'Ow would you l*i*ke men to st'y at 'ome and do the fam'ly wash*i*n'?"

(*Laughter.*)

I told 'im I wouldn't advise it. I 'ave too much respect fur—me clo'es.

VAGRANT. It's their place—the women ought to do the washin'

MR. P. I'm not sure you ain't right. For a good many o' you fellas, from the look o' you—you cawn't even wash yerselves.

(*Laughter.*)

VOICE (*threatening*). 'Oo are you talkin' to?

(*Chairman more anxious than before—movement in the crowd.*)

THREATENING VOICE. Which of us d'you mean?

MR. P. (*coolly looking down.*) Well, it takes about ten of your sort to myke a man, so you may take it I mean the lot of you.

(*Angry indistinguishable retorts and the crowd sways.* MISS ERNESTINE BLUNT, *who has been watching the fray with serious face, turns suddenly, catching sight of some one just arrived at the end of the platform.* MISS BLUNT *goes* R. *with alacrity, saying audibly to* PILCHER *as she passes, "Here she is," and proceeds to offer her hand helping some one to get up the improvised steps. Laughter and interruption in the crowd.*)

LADY JOHN. Now, there's another woman going to speak.

JEAN. Oh, is she? Who? Which? I do hope she'll be one of the wild ones.

MR. P. (*speaking through this last. Glancing at the new arrival whose hat appears above the platform*

R.). That's all right, then. (*Turns to the left.*) When I've attended to this microbe that's vitiating the air on my right——

(*Laughter and interruptions from the crowd.*)

STONOR (*staring* R., *one dazed instant, at the face of the new arrival, his own changes*).

(JEAN *withdraws her arm from his and quite suddenly presses a shade nearer the platform.* STONOR *moves forward and takes her by the arm.*)

We're going now.

JEAN. Not yet—oh, please not yet. (*Breathless, looking back.*) Why I—I do believe——

STONOR (*to* LADY JOHN, *with decision*). I'm going to take JEAN out of this mob. Will you come?

LADY JOHN. What? Oh yes, if you think—— (*Another look through her glasses.*) But isn't that —*surely* its——!!!

(VIDA LEVERING *comes forward* R. *She wears a long, plain, dark green dust-cloak. Stands talking to* ERNESTINE BLUNT *and glancing a little apprehensively at the crowd.*)

JEAN. Geoffrey!

STONOR (*trying to draw* JEAN *away*). Lady John's tired——

JEAN. But you don't see who it is, Geoffrey——! (*Looks into his face, and is arrested by the look she finds there.*)

(LADY JOHN *has pushed in front of them amazed, transfixed, with glass up.* GEOFFREY STONOR *restrains a gesture of annoy-*

ance, and withdraws behind two big policemen. JEAN *from time to time turns to look at him with a face of perplexity.*)

MR. P. (*resuming through a fire of indistinct interruption*). I'll come down and attend to that microbe while a lady will say a few words to you (*raises his voice*)—if she can myke 'erself 'eard.

(PILCHER *retires in the midst of booing and cheers.*)

CHAIRMAN (*harassed and trying to create a diversion*). Some one suggests—and it's such a good idea I'd like you to listen to it—

(*Noise dies down.*)

that a clause shall be inserted in the next Suffrage Bill that shall expressly reserve to each Cabinet Minister, and to any respectable man, the power to prevent the Franchise being given to the female members of his family on his public declaration of their lack of sufficient intelligence to entitle them to vote.

VOICES. Oh! oh!

CHAIRMAN. Now, I ask you to listen, as quietly as you can, to a lady who is not accustomed to speaking—a—in Trafalgar Square—or a . . . as a matter of fact, at all.

VOICES. "A dumb lady." "Hooray!" "Three cheers for the dumb lady!"

CHAIRMAN. A lady who, as I've said, will tell you, if you'll behave yourselves, her impressions of the administration of police-court justice in this country.

(JEAN *looks wondering at* STONOR'S *sphinx-like face as* VIDA LEVERING *comes to the edge of the platform.*)

MISS L. Mr. Chairman, men and women——

VOICES (*off*). Speak up.

(*She flushes, comes quite to the edge of the platform and raises her voice a little.*)

MISS L. I just wanted to tell you that I was—I was—present in the police-court when the women were charged for creating a disturbance.

VOICE. Y' oughtn't t' get mixed up in wot didn't concern you.

MISS L. I—I—— (*Stumbles and stops.*)

(*Talking and laughing increases.* "Wot's 'er name?" "Mrs. or Miss?" "Ain't seen this one before.")

CHAIRMAN (*anxiously*). Now, see here, men; don't interrupt——

A GIRL (*shrilly*). I like this one's *'at*. Ye can see she ain't one of 'em.

MISS L. (*trying to recommence*). I——

VOICE. They're a disgrace—them women be'ind yer.

A MAN WITH A FATHERLY AIR. It's the w'y they goes on as mykes the Government keep ye from gettin' yer rights.

CHAIRMAN (*losing his temper*). It's the way *you* go on that——

(*Noise increases.* CHAIRMAN *drowned, waves his arms and moves his lips.* MISS LEVERING *discouraged, turns and looks at* ERNESTINE BLUNT *and pantomimes "It's no good. I can't go on."* ERNESTINE BLUNT *comes forward, says a word to the* CHAIRMAN, *who ceases gyrating, and nods.*)

MISS E. B. (*facing the crowd*). Look here. If the Government withhold the vote because they don't like the way some of us ask for it—*let them give it to the Quiet Ones*. Does the Government want to punish *all* women because they don't like the manners of a handful? Perhaps that's you men's notion of just*i*ce. It *i*sn't women's.

VOICES. Haw! haw!

MISS L. Yes. Th-this is the first time I've ever "gone on," as you call it, but they never gave me a vote.

MISS E. B. (*with energy*). No! And there are one—two—three—four women on this platform. Now, we all want the vote, as you know. Well, we'd agree to be disfranch*i*sed all our l*i*ves, if they'd give the vote to all the other women.

VOICE. Look here, you made one speech, give the lady a chawnce.

MISS E. B. (*retires smiling*). That's *just* what I wanted *you* to do!

MISS L. Perhaps you—you don't know—you don't know——

VOICE (*sarcastic*). 'Ow 're we goin' to know if you can't tell us?

MISS L. (*flushing and smiling*). Thank you for that. We couldn't have a better motto. How *are* you to know *i*f we can't somehow manage to tell you? (*With a visible effort she goes on.*) Well, I certainly didn't know before that the sergeants and pol*i*cemen are *i*nstructed to deceive the people as to the time such cases are heard. You ask, and you're sent to Marlborough Police Court instead of to Marylebone.

VOICE. They ought ter sent yer to 'Olloway—do y' good.

OLD NEWSVENDOR. You go on, Miss, don't mind 'im.

VOICE. Wot d'yon expect from a pig but a grunt?

MISS L. You're told the case will be at two o'clock, and it's really called for eleven. Well, I took a great deal of trouble, and I didn't believe what I was told—

(*Warming a little to her task.*)

Yes, that's almost the first thing we have to learn—to get over our touching faith that, because a man tells us something, it's true. I got to the right court, and I was so anxious not to be late, I was too early. The case before the Women's was just coming on. I heard a noise. At the door I saw the helmets of two policemen, and I said to myself: "What sort of crime shall I have to sit and hear about? Is this a burglar coming along between the two big policemen, or will it be a murderer? What sort of felon is to stand in the dock before the women whose crime is they ask for the vote?" But, try as I would, I couldn't see the prisoner. My heart misgave me. Is it a woman, I wondered? Then the policemen got nearer, and I saw—(*she waits an instant*)—a little, thin, half-starved boy. What do you think he was charged with? Stealing. What had he been stealing—that small criminal? *Milk.* It seemed to me as I sat there looking on, that the men who had the affairs of the world in their hands from the beginning, and who've made so poor a business of it——

VOICES. Oh! oh! Pore benighted man! Are we down-'earted? *Oh*, no!

MISS L. —so poor a business of it as to have the poor and the unemployed in the condition they' e in to-day—when your only remedy for a starving child is to hale him off to the police-court—because he had managed to get a little milk—well, I *did* wonder that the men refuse to be helped with a problem they've so notoriously failed at. I began to say to myself: "Isn't it time the women lent a hand?"

A VOICE. Would you have women magistrates?

(*She is stumped by the suddenness of the demand.*)

VOICES. Haw! Haw! Magistrates!

ANOTHER. Women! Let 'em prove first they deserve——

A SHABBY ART STUDENT (*his hair longish, soft hat, and flowing tie*). They study music by thousands; where's their Beethoven? Where's their Plato? Where's the woman Shakespeare?

ANOTHER. Yes—what 'a' they ever *done*?

(*The speaker clenches her hands, and is recovering her presence of mind, so that by the time the* CHAIRMAN *can make himself heard with, "Now men, give this lady a fair hearing—don't interrupt"—she, with the slightest of gestures, waves him aside with a low "It's all right."*)

MISS L. (*steadying and raising her voice*). These questions are quite proper! They are often asked elsewhere; and I would like to ask in return: Since when was human society held to exist for its handful of geniuses? How many Platos are there here in this crowd?

A VOICE (*very loud and shrill*). Divil a wan!

(*Laughter.*)

MISS L. Not one. Yet that doesn't keep you men off the register. How many Shakespeares are there in all England to-day? Not one. Yet the State doesn't tumble to pieces. Railroads and ships are built —homes are kept going, and babies are born. The world goes on! (*bending over the crowd*) It goes on *by virtue of its common people.*

VOICES (*subdued*). Hear! hear!

MISS L. I am not concerned that you should think we women can paint great pictures, or compose immortal music, or write good books. I am content that we should be classed with the common people—who keep the world going. But (*straightening up and taking a fresh start*), I'd like the world to go a great deal better. We were talking about justice. I have been inquiring into the kind of lodging the poorest class of homeless women can get in this town of London. I find that only the men of that class are provided for. Some measure to establish Rowton Houses for women has been before the London County Council. They looked into the question "very carefully," so their apologists say. And what did they decide? They decided that *they could do nothing.*

LADY JOHN (*having forced her way to* STONOR'S *side*). Is that true?

STONOR (*speaking through* MISS LEVERING'S *next words*). I don't know.

MISS L. Why could that great, all-powerful body do nothing? Because, if these cheap and decent houses were opened, they said, the homeless women in the streets would make use of them! You'll think I'm not in earnest. But that was actually the decision and the reason given for it. Women that the bitter struggle for existence has forced into a life of horror——

STONOR (*sternly to* LADY JOHN). You think this is the kind of thing—— (*A motion of the head towards* JEAN.)

MISS L. —the outcast women might take advantage of the shelter these decent, cheap places offered. But the *men*, I said! Are all who avail themselves of Lord Rowton's hostels, are *they* all angels? Or does wrong-doing in a man not matter? Yet women are recommended to depend on the chivalry of men.

(*The two policemen, who at first had been strolling about, have stood during this scene in front of* GEOFFREY STONOR. *They turn now and walk away, leaving* STONOR *exposed. He, embarrassed, moves uneasily, and* VIDA LEVERING'S *eye falls upon his big figure. He still has the collar of his motor coat turned up to his ears. A change passes over her face, and her nerve fails her an instant.*)

MISS L. Justice and chivalry!! (*she steadies her voice and hurries on*)—they both remind me of what those of you who read the police-court news—(I have begun only lately to do that)—but you've seen the accounts of the girl who's been tried in Manchester lately for the murder of her child. Not pleasant reading. Even if we'd noticed it, we wouldn't speak of it in my world. A few months ago I should have turned away my eyes and forgotten even the headline as quickly as I could. But since that morning in the police-court, I read these things. This, as you'll remember, was about a little working girl—an orphan of eighteen—who crawled with the dead body of her new-born child to her master's back-door, and left the baby there. She dragged herself a little way off and fainted. A few days later she found herself in court, being tried for the murder of her child. Her master—a married man—had of course reported the "find" at his back-door to the police, and he had been summoned to give evidence. The girl cried out to him in the open court, "You are the father!" He couldn't deny it. The Coroner at the jury's request censured the man, and regretted that the law didn't make him responsible. But he went scot-free. And that girl is now serving her sentence in Strangeways Gaol.

(*Murmuring and scraps of indistinguishable comment in the crowd, through which only* JEAN'S *voice is clear.*)

JEAN (*who has wormed her way to* STONOR'S *side*). Why do you dislike her so?

STONOR. I? Why should you think——

JEAN (*with a vaguely frightened air*). I never saw you look as you did—as you do.

CHAIRMAN. Order, please—give the lady a fair——

MISS L. (*signing to him "It's all right"*). Men make boast that an English citizen is tried by his peers. What woman is tried by hers?

(*A sombre passion strengthens her voice and hurries her on.*)

A woman is arrested by a man, brought before a man judge, tried by a jury of men, condemned by men, taken to prison by a man, and by a man she's hanged! Where *in* all this were *her* "peers"? Why did men so long ago insist on trial by "a jury of their peers"? So that just*ice* shouldn't miscarry—wasn't it? A man's peers would best understand his circumstances, his temptation, the degree of his guilt. Yet there's no such unlikeness between different classes of men as exists between man and woman. What man has the knowledge that makes him a fit judge of woman's deeds at that time of anguish—that hour—(*lowers her voice and bends over the crowd*)—that hour that some woman struggled through to put each man here into the world. I noticed when a previous speaker quoted the Labour Party you applauded. Some of you here—I gather—call yourselves Labour men. Every woman who has borne a child is a Labour woman. No man among you can judge what she goes through in her hour of darkness——

JEAN (*with frightened eyes on her lover's set, white face, whispers*). Geoffrey——

MISS L (*catching her fluttering breath, goes on very low*) —in that great agony when, even under the best conditions that money and devotion can buy, many a woman falls into temporary mania, and not a few go down to death. In the case of this poor little abandoned working girl, what man can be the fit judge of her deeds in that awful moment of half-crazed temptation? Women know of these things as those know burning who have walked through fire.

(STONOR *makes a motion towards* JEAN *and she turns away fronting the audience. Her hands go up to her throat as though she suffered a choking sensation. It is in her face that she "knows."* MISS LEVERING *leans over the platform and speaks with a low and thrilling earnestness.*)

I would say in conclusion to the women here, it's not

enough to be sorry for these our unfortunate *sisters*. We must get the condit*ions* of life made fairer. We women must organise. We must learn to work together. We have all (rich and poor, happy and unhappy) worked so long and so exclusively for *men*, we hardly know how to work for one another. But we must learn. Those who can, may *give* money——

VOICES (*grumbling*). Oh, yes—Money! Money!

MISS L. Those who haven't pennies to *give*—even those people aren't so poor they can't *give* some part of their labour—some share of the*ir* sympathy and support.

(*Turns to hear something the* CHAIRMAN *is whispering to her.*)

JEAN (*low to* LADY JOHN). Oh, I'm glad I've got power!

LADY JOHN (*bewildered*). Power!—*you?*

JEAN. Yes, all that money——

(LADY JOHN *tries to make her way to* STONOR.)

MISS L. (*suddenly turning from the* CHAIRMAN *to the crowd*). Oh, yes, I hope you'll all join the Un*i*on. Come up after the meeting and give your names.

LOUD VOICE. You won't get many men.

MISS L. (*with fire*). Then it's to the women I appeal!

(*She is about to retire when, with a sudden gleam in her lit eyes, she turns for the last time to the crowd, silencing the general murmur and holding the people by the sudden concentration of passion in her face.*)

I don't mean to say it wouldn't be better if men and women did th*i*s work together—shoulder to shoulder.

But the mass of men won't have it so. I only hope they'll real*i*se in time the good they've renounced and the spirit they've aroused. For I know as well as any man could tell me, it would be a bad day for England if all women felt about all men *as I do.*

(*She retires in a tumult. The others on the platform close about her. The* CHAIRMAN *tries in vain to get a hearing from the excited crowd.*)

(JEAN *tries to make her way through the knot of people surging round her.*)

STONOR (*calls*). Here!—Follow me!

JEAN. No—no—I——

STONOR. You're going the wrong way.

JEAN. *This* is the way I must go.

STONOR. You can get out qu*i*cker on th*i*s s*i*de.

JEAN. I don't *want* to get out.

STONOR. What! Where are you going?

JEAN. To ask that woman to let me have the honour of work*i*ng w*i*th her.

(*She disappears in the crowd.*)

CURTAIN.

ACT III

SCENE: *The drawing-room at old* MR. DUNBARTON'S *house in Eaton Square. Six o'clock the same evening. As the Curtain rises the door* (L.) *opens and* JEAN *appears on the threshold. She looks back into her own sitting-room, then crosses the drawing-room, treading softly on the parquet spaces between the rugs. She goes to the window and is in the act of parting the lace curtains when the folding doors* (C.) *are opened by the* BUTLER.

JEAN (*to the Servant*). Sh!

(*She goes softly back to the door she has left open and closes it carefully. When she turns, the* BUTLER *has stepped aside to admit* GEOFFREY STONOR, *and departed, shutting the folding doors.* STONOR *comes rapidly forward.*)

(*Before he gets a word out.*) Speak low, please.

STONOR (*angrily*). I waited about a whole hour for you to come back.

(JEAN *turns away as though vaguely looking for the nearest chair.*)

If you didn't mind leaving *me* like that, you might have considered Lady John.

JEAN (*pausing*). Is she here with you?

STONOR. No. My place was nearer than this, and she was very tired. I left her to get some tea. We couldn't tell whether you'd be here, or *what* had become of you.

JEAN. Mr. Trent got us a hansom.

STONOR. Trent?

JEAN. The Chairman of the meeting.

STONOR. "Got us ——"?

JEAN. Miss Levering and me.

STONOR (*incensed*). MISS L ——

BUTLER (*opens the door and announces*) Mr. Farnborough.

(*Enter* MR. RICHARD FARNBOROUGH—*more flurried than ever.*)

FARN. (*seeing* STONOR). At last! You'll forgive this incursion, Miss Dunbarton, when you hear—— (*Turns abruptly back to* STONOR.) They've been telegraphing you all over London. In despair they set me on your track.

STONOR. Who did? What's up?

FARN. (*lays down his hat and fumbles agitatedly in his breast-pocket*). There was the devil to pay at Dutfield last night. The Liberal chap tore down from London and took over your meeting!

STONOR. Oh?—Nothing about it in the Sunday paper *I* saw.

FARN. Wait till you see the Press to-morrow morning! There was a great rally and the beggar made a rousing speech.

STONOR. What about?

FARN. Abolition of the Upper House——

STONOR. They were at that when I was at Eton!

FARN. Yes. But this new man has got a way of putting things!—the people went mad. (*Pompously.*) The Liberal platform as defined at Dutfield is going to make a big difference

STONOR (*drily*). You think so.

FARN. Well, your agent says as much. (*Opens telegram.*)

STONOR. My—— (*Taking telegram.*) "Try find Stonor"—Hm! Hm!

FARN. (*pointing*). —"tremendous effect of last night's Liberal manifesto ought to be counteracted in to-morrow's papers." (*Very earnestly.*) You see, Mr. Stonor, it's a battle-cry we want.

STONOR (*turns on his heel*). Claptrap!

FARN. (*a little dashed*). Well, they've been saying we have nothing to offer but personal popularity. No practical reform. No——

STONOR. No truckling to the masses, I suppose. (*Walks impatiently away.*)

FARN. (*snubbed*). Well, in these democratic days—— (*Turns to* JEAN *for countenance.*) I hope you'll forgive my bursting in like this. (*Struck by her face.*) But I can see you realise the gravity—— (*Lowering his voice with an air of speaking for her ear alone.*) It isn't as if he were going to be a mere private member. Everybody knows he'll be in the Cabinet.

STONOR (*drily*). It may be a Liberal Cabinet.

FARN. Nobody thought so up to last night. Why, even your brother—but I am afraid I'm seeming officious. (*Takes up his hat.*)

STONOR (*coldly*). What about my brother?

FARN. I met Lord Windlesham as I rushed out of the Carlton.

STONOR. Did he say anything?

FARN. I told him the Dutfield news.

STONOR (*impatiently*). Well?

FARN. He said it only confirmed his fears.

STONOR (*half under his breath*). Said that, did he?

FARN. Yes. Defeat is inevitable, he thinks, unless—— (*Pause.*)

(GEOFFREY STONOR, *who has been pacing the floor, stops but doesn't raise his eyes.*)

unless you can "manufacture some political dynamite within the next few hours." Those were his words.

STONOR (*resumes his walking to and fro, raises his head and catches sight of* JEAN'S *white, drawn face. Stops short*). You are very tired.

JEAN. No. No.

STONOR (*to* FARNBOROUGH). I'm obliged to you for taking so much trouble. (*Shakes hands by way of dismissing* FARNBOROUGH.) I'll see what can be done.

FARN. (*offering the reply-paid form*). If you'd like to wire I'll take it.

STONOR (*faintly amused*). You don't understand, my young friend. Moves of this kind are not rushed at by responsible politicians. I must have time for consideration.

FARN. (*disappointed*). Oh, well, I only hope someone else won't jump into the breach before you—(*Watch in hand*) I tell you. (*To* JEAN.) I'll find out what time the newspapers go to press on Sunday. Good-bye. (*To* STONOR.) I'll be at the Club just *in case* I can be of any use.

STONOR (*firmly*). No, don't do that. If I should have anything new to say——

FARN. (*feverishly*). B-b-but with our party, as your brother said—"heading straight for a vast electoral disaster——"

STONOR. If I decide on a counterblast I shall simply telegraph to headquarters. Goodbye.

FARN. Oh—a—g-goodbye. (*A gesture of "The country's going to the dogs."*)

(JEAN *rings the bell.* *Exit* FARNBOROUGH.)

STONOR (*studying the carpet*). "Political dynamite," eh? (*Pause.*) After all . . . women are much more conservative than men—aren't they?

(JEAN *looks straight in front of her, making no attempt to reply.*)

Especially the women the property qualification would bring in. (*He glances at* JEAN *as though for the first time conscious of her silence.*) You see now (*he throws himself into the chair by the table*) one reason why I've encouraged you to take an interest in public affairs. Because people like us don't go screaming about it, is no sign we don't (some of us) see what's on the way. However little they want to, women of our class will have to come into line. All the best things in the world—everything that civilisation has won will be in danger if—when this change comes—the only women who have practical political training are the women of the lower classes. Women of the lower classes, and (*his brows knit heavily*)—women inoculated by the Socialist virus.

JEAN. Geoffrey.

STONOR (*draws the telegraph form towards him*). Let

us see, how we shall put it—when the time comes—shall we? (*He detaches a pencil from his watch chain and bends over the paper, writing.*)

(JEAN *opens her lips to speak, moves a shade nearer the table and then falls back upon her silent, half-incredulous misery.*)

STONOR (*holds the paper off, smiling*). Enough dynamite in that! Rather too much, isn't there, little girl?

JEAN. Geoffrey, I know her story.

STONOR. Whose story?

JEAN. Miss Levering's.

STONOR. *Whose?*

JEAN. Vida Levering's.

(STONOR *stares speechless. Slight pause.*)

(*The words escaping from her in a miserable cry*) Why did you desert her?

STONOR (*staggered.*) I? *I?*

JEAN. Oh, why did you do it?

STONOR (*bewildered*). What in the name of—— What has she been saying to you?

JEAN. Some one else told me part. Then the way you looked when you saw her at Aunt Ellen's—Miss Levering's saying you didn't know her—then your letting out that you knew even the curious name on the handkerchief—— Oh, I pieced it together——

STONOR (*with recovered self-possession*). Your ingenuity is undeniable!

JEAN —and then, when she said that at the meeting about "the dark hour" and I looked at your face—it flashed over me—— Oh, *why* did you desert her?

STONOR. I *didn't* desert her.

JEAN. Ah-h! (*Puts her hands before her eyes.*)

(STONOR *makes a passionate motion towards her, is checked by her muffled voice saying*)

I'm glad—I'm glad!

(*He stares bewildered.* JEAN *drops her hands in her lap and steadies her voice.*)

She went away from you, then?

STONOR. You don't expect me to enter into——

JEAN. She went away from you?

STONOR (*with a look of almost uncontrollable anger*). Yes!

JEAN. Was that because you wouldn't marry her?

STONOR. I couldn't marry her—and she knew it.

JEAN. Did you want to?

STONOR (*an instant's angry scrutiny and then turning away his eyes*). I thought I did—*then.* It's a long time ago.

JEAN. And why "couldn't" you?

STONOR (*a movement of strong irritation cut short*). Why are you catechising me? It's a matter that concerns another woman.

JEAN. If you're saying that it doesn't concern me, you're saying—(*her lip trembles*)—that *you* don't concern me.

STONOR (*commanding his temper with difficulty*). In those days I—I was absolutely dependent on my father.

JEAN. Why, you must have been thirty, Geoffrey.

STONOR (*slight pause*). What? Oh—thereabouts.

JEAN. And everybody says you're so clever.

STONOR. Well, everybody's mistaken.

JEAN (*drawing nearer*). It must have been terribly hard——

(STONOR *turns towards her.*)

for you both—

(*He arrests his movement and stands stonily.*)

that a man like you shouldn't have had the freedom that even the lowest seem to have.

STONOR. Freedom?

JEAN. To marry the woman they choose.

STONOR. She didn't break off our relations because I couldn't marry her.

JEAN. Why was it, then?

STONOR. You're too young to discuss such a story. (*Half turns away.*)

JEAN. I'm not so young as she was when——

STONOR (*wheeling upon her*). Very well, then, if you will have it! The truth is, it didn't seem to weigh upon her, as it seems to on you, that I wasn't able to marry her.

JEAN. Why are you so sure of that?

STONOR. Because she didn't so much as hint such a thing when she wrote that she meant to break off the—the——

JEAN. What made her write like that?

STONOR (*with suppressed rage*). Why *will* you go on talking of what's so long over and ended?

JEAN. What reason did she give?

STONOR. If your curiosity has so got the upper hand —*ask her.*

JEAN (*her eyes upon him*). You're afraid to tell me.

STONOR (*putting pressure on himself to answer quietly*). I still hoped—at *that* time—to win my father over. She blamed me because (*goes to window and looks blindly out and speaks in a low tone*) if the child had lived it wouldn't have been possible to get my father to—to overlook it.

JEAN (*faintly*). You wanted it *overlooked?* I don't underst——

STONOR (*turning passionately back to her*). Of course you don't. (*He seizes her hand and tries to draw her to him.*) If you did, you wouldn't be the beautiful, tender, innocent child you are——

JEAN (*has withdrawn her hand and shrunk from him with an impulse—slight as is its expression—so tragically eloquent, that fear for the first time catches hold of him*). I am glad you didn't mean to desert her, Geoffrey. It wasn't your fault after all—only some misunderstanding that can be cleared up.

STONOR. *Cleared up?*

JEAN. Yes. Cleared up.

STONOR (*aghast*). You aren't thinking that this miserable old affair I'd as good as forgotten——

JEAN (*in a horror-struck whisper, with a glance at the door which he doesn't see*). *Forgotten!*

STONOR. No, no. I don't mean exactly forgotten. But you're torturing me so I don't know what I'm saying. (*He goes closer.*) You aren't—Jean! you—you aren't going to let it come between you and me!

JEAN (*presses her handkerchief to her lips, and then, taking it away, answers steadily*). I can't make or unmake what's past. But I'm glad, at least, that you didn't *mean* to desert her in her trouble. You'll remind her of that first of all, won't you? (*Moves to the door,* L.)

STONOR. Where are you going? (*Raising his voice.*) Why should I remind anybody of what I want only to forget?

JEAN (*finger on lip*). Sh!

STONOR (*with eyes on the door*). You don't mean that *she's*——

JEAN. Yes. I left her to get a little rest.

(*He recoils in an access of uncontrollable rage. She follows him. Speechless, he goes down* R. *to get his hat.*)

Geoffrey, don't go before you hear me. I don't know if what I think matters to you now—but I hope it does. (*With tears.*) You can still make me think of you *w*ithout shrink*i*ng—if you will.

STONOR (*fixes her a moment with his eyes. Then sternly*). What is it you are asking of me?

JEAN. To make amends, Geoffrey.

STONOR (*with an outburst*). You poor l*i*ttle *i*nnocent!

JEAN. I'm poor enough. But (*locking her hands together*) I'm not so *i*nnocent but what I know you must right that old wrong now, *i*f you're ever to right it.

STONOR. You aren't *i*nsane enough to think I would turn round *i*n these few hours and go back to someth*i*ng that ten years ago was ended for ever! Why, it's stark, star*i*ng madness!

JEAN. No. (*Catching on his arm.*) What you did ten years ago—*that* was mad. This is paying a debt.

STONOR. Look here, Jean, you're dreadfully wrought up and excited—t*i*red too——

JEAN. No, not t*i*red—though I've travelled so far to-day. I know you smile at sudden convers*i*ons. You think they're hyster*i*cal—worse—vulgar. But people must get their revelat*i*on how they can. And, Geoffrey, *i*f I can't make you see this one of mine—I shall know your love could never mean strength to me. Only weakness. And I shall be afraid. So afraid I'll never dare to give you the *chance* of making me loathe myself. I shall never see you again.

STONOR. How right *I* was to be afraid of that vein of fanaticism in you. (*Moves towards the door.*)

JEAN. Certainly you couldn't make a greater mistake than to go away now and think it any good ever to come back. (*He turns.*) Even if I came to feel different, I couldn't *do* anything different. I should know all this couldn't be forgotten. I should know that it would poison my life in the end. Yours too.

STONOR (*with suppressed fury*). She has made good use of her time! (*With a sudden thought.*) What has changed her? Has *she* been seeing visions too?

JEAN. What do you mean?

STONOR. Why is she intriguing to get hold of a man that, ten years ago, she flatly refused to see, or hold any communication with?

JEAN. "Intriguing to get hold of?" She hasn't mentioned you!

STONOR. *What!* Then how in the name of Heaven do you know—that she wants—what you ask?

JEAN (*firmly*). There can't be any doubt about that.

STONOR (*with immense relief*). You absurd, ridiculous child! Then all this is just your own unaided invention. Well—I could thank God! (*Falls into the nearest chair and passes his handkerchief over his face.*)

JEAN (*perplexed, uneasy*). For what are you thanking God?

STONOR (*trying to think out his plan of action*). Suppose—(I'm not going to risk it)—but suppose—(*He looks up and at the sight of* JEAN'S *face a new tenderness comes into his own. He rises suddenly.*) Whether I deserve to suffer or not—it's quite certain *you* don't. Don't cry, dear one. It never was the real thing. I had to wait till I knew you before I understood.

JEAN (*lifts her eyes brimming*). Oh, is that true? (*Checks her movement towards him.*) Loving you has made things clear to me I didn't dream of before. If I could think that because of me you were able to do this——

STONOR (*seizes her by the shoulders and says hoarsely*). Look here! Do you seriously ask me to give up the girl I love—to go and offer to marry a woman that even to think of——

JEAN. You cared for her once. You'll care about her again. She is beautiful and brilliant—everything. I've heard she could win any man she set herself to——

. STONOR (*pushing* JEAN *from him*). She's bewitched you!

JEAN. Geoffrey, Geoffrey, you aren't going away lik that. This isn't *the end!*

STONOR (*darkly—hesitating*). I suppose even if she refused me, you'd——

JEAN. She won't refuse you.

STONOR. She did once.

JEAN. She didn't refuse to *marry* you——

(JEAN *is going to the door* L.)

STONOR (*catches her by the arm*) Wait!—a——(*Hunting for some means of gaining time.*) Lady John is waiting all this while for the car to go back with a message.

JEAN. *That's* not a matter of life and death——

STONOR. All the same—I'll go down and give the order.

JEAN (*stopping quite still on a sudden*). Very well. (*Sits* C.) You'll come back if you're the man I pray you are. (*Breaks into a flood of silent tears, her elbows on the table* (C.) *her face in her hands.*)

STONOR (*returns, bends over her, about to take her in his arms*). Dearest of all the world——

(*Door* L. *opens softly and* VIDA LEVERING *appears. She is arrested at sight of* STONOR, *and is in the act of drawing back when, upon the slight noise,* STONOR *looks round. His face darkens, he stands staring at her and then with a look of speechless anger goes silently out* C. JEAN, *hearing him shut the door, drops her head on the table with a sob.* VIDA LEVERING *crosses slowly to her and stands a moment silent at the girl's side.*)

MISS L. What is the matter?

JEAN (*lifting her head and drying her eyes*). I—I've been seeing Geoffrey.

MISS L. (*with an attempt at lightness*). Is this the effect seeing Geoffrey has?

JEAN. You see, I know now (*as* MISS LEVERING *looks quite uncomprehending*)—how he (*drops her eyes*)—how he spoiled some one else's life.

MISS L. (*quickly*). Who tells you that?

JEAN. Several people have told me.

MISS L. Well, you should be very careful how you believe what you hear.

JEAN (*passionately*). You *know* it's true.

MISS L. I know that it's possible to be mistaken.

JEAN. I see! You're trying to shield him——

MISS L. Why should I—what is it to me?

JEAN (*with tears*). Oh—h, how you must love him!

MISS L. Listen to me——

JEAN (*rising*). What's the use of your going on denying it?

(MISS LEVERING, *about to break in, is silenced.*) *Geoffrey doesn't.*

(JEAN, *struggling to command her feelings, goes to window.* VIDA LEVERING *relinquishes an impulse to follow, and sits left centre.* JEAN *comes slowly back with her eyes bent on the floor, does not lift them till she is quite near* VIDA. *Then the girl's self-absorbed face changes.*)

Oh, don't look like that! I shall bring him back to you! (*Drops on her knees beside the other's chair.*)

MISS L. You would be impertinent (*softening*) if you weren't a romantic child. You can't bring him back.

JEAN. Yes, he——

MISS L. But there's something you *can* do——

JEAN. What?

MISS L. Bring him to the point where he recognises that he's in our debt.

JEAN. In *our* debt?

MISS L. In debt to women. He can't repay the one he robbed——

JEAN (*wincing and rising from her knees*). Yes, yes.

MISS L. (*sternly*). No, he can't repay the dead. But there are the living. There are the thousands with hope still in their hearts and youth in their blood. Let him help *them*. Let him be a Friend to Women.

JEAN (*rising on a wave of enthusiasm*). Yes, yes—I understand. That too!

(*The door opens. As* STONOR *enters with* LADY JOHN, *he makes a slight gesture towards the two as much as to say*, "*You see.*")

JEAN (*catching sight of him*). Thank you!

LADY JOHN (*in a clear, commonplace tone to* JEAN). Well, you rather gave us the slip. Vida, I believe Mr. Stonor wants to see you for a few minutes (*glances at watch*)—but I'd like a word with you first, as I must get back. (*To* STONOR.) Do you think the car—your man said something about re-charging.

STONOR (*hastily*). Oh, did he?—I'll see about it.

(*As* STONOR *is going out he encounters the* BUTLER. *Exit* STONOR.)

BUTLER. Mr. Trent has called, Miss, to take Miss Levering to the meeting.

JEAN. Bring Mr. Trent into my sitting-room. I'll tell him—you can't go to-night.

[*Exeunt* BUTLER C., JEAN L.

LADY JOHN (*hurriedly*). I know, my dear, *you're* not aware of what that impulsive girl wants to insist on.

MISS L. Yes, I am aware of it.

LADY JOHN. But it isn't with your sanction, surely, that she goes on making this extraordinary demand.

MISS L. (*slowly*). I didn't sanction it at first, but I've been thinking it over.

LADY JOHN. Then all I can say is I am greatly disappointed in you. You threw this man over years ago for reasons—whatever they were—that seemed to you good and sufficient. And now you come between him and a younger woman—just to play Nemesis, so far as I can make out!

MISS L. Is that what he says?

LADY JOHN. He says nothing that isn't fair and considerate.

MISS L. I can see he's changed.

LADY JOHN. And you're unchanged—is that it?

MISS L. I've changed even more than he.

LADY JOHN. But (*pity and annoyance blended in her tone*)—you care about him still, Vida?

MISS L. No.

LADY JOHN. I see. It's just that you wish to marry somebody——

MISS L. Oh, Lady John, there are no men listening.

LADY JOHN (*surprised*). No, I didn't suppose there were.

MISS L. Then why keep up that old pretence?

LADY JOHN. What pre——

MISS L. That to marry *at all costs* is every woman's dearest ambition till the grave closes over her. You and I *know* it isn't true.

LADY JOHN. Well, but—— Oh! it was just the unexpected sight of him bringing it back—— *That* was what fired you this afternoon! (*With an honest attempt at sympathetic understanding.*) Of course. The memory of a thing like that can never die—can never even be dimmed—*for the woman.*

MISS L. I mean her to th*i*nk so.

LADY JOHN (*bewildered*). Jean!

(MISS LEVERING *nods*.)

LADY JOHN. And it *isn't* so?

MISS L. You don't seriously believe a woman w*i*th anyth*i*ng else to th*i*nk about, comes to the end of ten years still *absorbed* in a memory of that sort?

LADY JOHN (*astonished*). You've got over it, then!

MISS L. If the newspapers didn't remind me I shouldn't remember once a twelvemonth that there was ever such a person as Geoffrey Stonor in the world.

LADY JOHN (*with unconscious rapture*). Oh, I'm *so* glad!

MISS L. (*smiles grimly*). Yes, I'm glad too.

LADY JOHN. And *if* Geoffrey Stonor offered you—what's called "reparation"—you'd refuse it?

MISS L. (*smiles a little contemptuously*). Geoffrey Stonor! For me he's simply one of the far-back links in a chain of evidence. It's certain I think a hundred times of other women's present unhappiness, to once that I remember that old unhappiness of mine that's past. I th*i*nk of the nail and chain makers of Cradley Heath. The sweated girls of the slums. I think of the army of ill-used women whose very existence I mustn't mention——

LADY JOHN (*interrupting hurriedly*). Then why in Heaven's name do you let poor Jean imag*i*ne——

MISS L. (*bending forward*). Look—I'll trust you, Lady John. I don't suffer from that old wrong as Jean thinks I do, but I shall co*i*n her sympathy into gold for a greater cause than mine.

H

LADY JOHN. I don't understand you.

MISS L. Jean isn't old enough to be able to care as much about a principle as about a person. But *if* my half-forgotten pain can turn her generosity into the common treasury——

LADY JOHN. What do you propose she shall do, poor child?

MISS L. Use her hold over Geoffrey Stonor to make him help us!

LADY JOHN. Help you?

MISS L. The man who served one woman—God knows how many more—very ill, shall serve hundreds of thousands well. Geoffrey Stonor shall make it harder for his son, harder still for his grandson, to treat any woman as he treated me.

LADY JOHN. How will he do that?

MISS L. By putting an end to the helplessness of women.

LADY JOHN (*ironically*). You must think he has a great deal of power——

MISS L. Power? Yes, men have too much over penniless and frightened women.

LADY JOHN (*impatiently*). What nonsense! You talk as though the women hadn't their share of human nature. *We* aren't made of ice any more than the men.

MISS L. No, but all the same we have more self-control.

LADY JOHN. Than men?

MISS L. You know we have.

LADY JOHN (*shrewdly*). I know we mustn't admit it.

MISS L. For fear they'd call us fishes!

LADY JOHN (*evasively*). They talk of our lack of

self-control—but it's the last thing they *want* women to have.

MISS L. Oh, we know what they want us to have. So we make shift to have it. If we don't, we go without hope—sometimes we go without bread.

LADY JOHN (*shocked*). Vida—do you mean to say that you ——

MISS L. I mean to say that men's vanity won't let them see it, but the thing's largely a question of economics.

LADY JOHN (*shocked*). You *never* loved him, then!

MISS L. Oh, yes, I loved him—*once*. It was my helplessness turned the best thing life can bring, into a curse for both of us.

LADY JOHN. I don't understand you ——

MISS L. Oh, being "understood!"—that's too much to expect. When people come to know I've joined the Union ——

LADY JOHN. But you won't ——

MISS L. —who is there who will resist the temptation to say, "Poor Vida Levering! What a pity she hasn't got a husband and a baby to keep her quiet"? The few who know about me, they'll be equally sure that it's not the larger view of life I've gained—my own poor little story is responsible for my new departure. (*Leans forward and looks into* LADY JOHN'S *face.*) My best friend, she will be surest of all, that it's a private sense of loss, or, lower yet, a grudge ——! But I tell you the only difference between me and thousands of women with husbands and babies is that I'm free to say what I think. *They aren't.*

LADY JOHN (*rising and looking at her watch*). I must get back—my poor ill-used guests.

MISS L. (*rising*). I won't ring. I think you'll find Mr. Stonor downstairs waiting for you.

LADY JOHN (*embarrassed*). Oh—a—he will have left word about the car in any case.

(MISS LEVERING *has opened the door* (C.). ALLEN TRENT *is in the act of saying goodbye to* JEAN *in the hall.*)

MISS L. Well, Mr. Trent, I didn't expect to see you this evening.

TRENT (*comes and stands in the doorway*). Why not? Have I ever failed?

MISS L. Lady John, this is one of our allies. He is good enough to squire me through the rabble from time to time.

LADY JOHN. Well, I think it's very handsome of you, after what she said to-day about men. (*Shakes hands.*)

TRENT. I've no great opinion of most men myself. I might add—or of most women.

LADY JOHN. Oh! Well, at any rate I shall go away relieved to think that Miss Levering's plain speaking hasn't alienated *all* masculine regard.

TRENT. Why should it?

LADY JOHN. That's right, Mr. Trent! Don't believe all she says in the heat of propaganda.

TRENT. I do believe all she says. But I'm not cast down.

LADY JOHN (*smiling*). Not when she says ——

TRENT (*interrupting*). Was there never a mysogynist of my sex who ended by deciding to make an exception?

LADY JOHN (*smiling significantly*). Oh, if *that's* what you build on!

TRENT. Well, why shouldn't a man-hater on your side prove equally open to reason?

MISS L. That part of the question doesn't concern me. I've come to a place where I realise that the first battles of this new campaign must be fought by women alone. The only effective help men could give —amendment of the law—they refuse. The rest is nothing.

LADY JOHN. Don't be ungrateful, Vida. Here's Mr. Trent ready to face criticism in publicly championing you.

MISS L. It's an illusion that I as an individual need Mr. Trent. I am quite safe in the crowd. Please don't wait for me, and don't come for me again.

TRENT (*flushes*). Of course if you'd rather——

MISS L. And that reminds me. I was asked to thank you and to tell you, too, that they—the women of the Union—they won't need your chairmanship any more—though that, I beg you to believe, has nothing to do with any feeling of mine.

TRENT (*hurt*). Of course, I know there must be other men ready—better known men——

MISS L. It isn't that. It's simply that they find a man can't keep a rowdy meeting in order as well as a woman.

(*He stares.*)

LADY JOHN. You aren't serious?

MISS L. (*to* TRENT). Haven't you noticed that all their worst disturbances come when men are in charge?

TRENT. Well—a—(*laughs a little ruefully as he moves to the door*) I hadn't connected the two ideas. Goodbye.

MISS L. Goodbye.

(JEAN *takes him downstairs, right centre.*)

LADY JOHN (*as* TRENT *disappears*). That nice boy's in love with you.

(MISS LEVERING *simply looks at her.*)

LADY JOHN. Goodbye. (*They shake hands.*) I wish you hadn't been so unkind to that nice boy!

MISS L. Do you?

LADY JOHN. Yes, for then I would be more certain of your telling Geoffrey Stonor that intelligent women don't nurse their wrongs and lie in wait to punish them.

MISS L. You are *not* certain?

LADY JOHN (*goes close up to* VIDA). Are you?

(VIDA *stands with her eyes on the ground, silent, motionless.* LADY JOHN, *with a nervous glance at her watch and a gesture of extreme perturbation, goes hurriedly out.* VIDA *shuts the door. She comes slowly back, sits down and covers her face with her hands. She rises and begins to walk up and down, obviously trying to master her agitation. Enter* GEOFFREY STONOR.)

MISS L. Well, have they primed you? Have you got your lesson (*with a little broken laugh*) *by heart* at last?

STONOR (*looking at her from immeasurable distance*). I am not sure I understand you. (*Pause.*) However unpropitious your mood may be—I shall discharge my errand. (*Pause. Her silence irritates him.*) I have promised to offer you what I bel*ie*ve is called "amends."

MISS L. (*quickly*). You've come to real*is*e, then—after all these years—that you owed me something?

STONOR (*on the brink of protest, checks himself*). I am not here to deny it.

MISS L. (*fiercely*). Pay, then—*pay*.

STONOR (*a moment's dread as he looks at her, his lips set. Then stonily*). I have prom*is*ed that, *i*f you exact it, I will.

MISS L. Ah! If I *ins*i*st* you'll "make it all good"! (*Quite low.*) Then don't you know you must pay me in kind?

STONOR. What do you mean.

MISS L. Give me back what you took from me: my old faith. Give me that.

STONOR. Oh, *i*f you mean to make phrases—— (*A gesture of scant patience.*)

MISS L. (*going closer*). Or give me back mere kindness—or even tolerance. Oh, I don't mean *your* tolerance! Give me back the power to think fairly of my brothers—not as mockers—thieves.

STONOR. I have not mocked you. And I have asked you——

MISS L. Something you knew I should refuse! Or (*her eyes blaze*) did you dare to be afraid I wouldn't?

STONOR. I suppose, if we set our teeth, we could——

MISS L. I couldn't—not even *i*f I set my teeth. And you wouldn't dream of asking me, *i*f you thought there was the smallest chance.

STONOR. I can do no more than make you an offer of such reparation as is in my power. If you don't accept it—— (*He turns with an air of "That's done."*)

MISS L. Accept it? No! . . . Go away and live in debt! Pay and pay and pay—and find yourself still in debt!—for a thing you'll never be able to give me back. (*Lower.*) And when you come to die, say to yourself, "I paid all creditors but one."

STONOR. I'm rather tired, you know, of this talk of debt. If I hear that you persist in it I shall have to——

MISS L. What? (*She faces him.*)

STONOR. No. I'll keep to my resolution. (*Turning to the door.*)

MISS L. (*intercepting him*). What resolution?

STONOR. I came here, under considerable pressure, to speak of the future—not to re-open the past.

MISS L. The Future and the Past are one.

STONOR. You talk as if that old madness was mine alone. It is the woman's way.

MISS L. I know. And it's not fair. Men suffer as well as we by the woman's starting wrong. We are taught to think the man a sort of demigod. If he tells her: "go down into Hell"—down into Hell she goes.

STONOR. Make no mistake. Not the woman alone. *They go down together.*

MISS L. Yes, they go down together, but the man comes up alone. As a rule. It is more convenient so —for him. And for the Other Woman.

(*The eyes of both go to* JEAN'S *door.*)

STONOR (*angrily*). My conscience is clear. I know —and so do you—that most men in my position wouldn't have troubled themselves. I gave myself endless trouble.

MISS L. (*with wondering eyes*). So you've gone about all these years feeling that you'd discharged every obligation.

STONOR. Not only that. I stood by you with a fidelity that was nothing short of Quixotic. If, woman like, you *must* recall the Past—I insist on your recalling it correctly.

MISS L. (*very low*). You think I don't recall it correctly?

STONOR. Not when you make—other people believe that I deserted you. (*With gathering wrath.*) It's a curious enough charge when you stop to consider—— (*Checks himself, and with a gesture of impatience sweeps the whole thing out of his way.*)

MISS L. Well, when we *do*—just for five minutes out of ten years—when we do stop to consider——

STONOR. We remember it was *you* who did the deserting! Since you had to rake the story up, you might have had the fairness to tell the facts.

MISS L. You think "the facts" would have excused you! (*She sits.*)

STONOR. No doubt you've forgotten them, since Lady John tells me you wouldn't remember my existence once a year if the newspapers didn't——

MISS L. Ah, you minded that!

STONOR (*with manly spirit*). I minded your giving false impressions. (*She is about to speak, he advances on her.*) Do you deny that you returned my letters unopened?

MISS L. (*quietly*). No.

STONOR. Do you deny that you refused to see me—and that, when I persisted, you vanished?

MISS L. I don't deny any of those things.

STONOR. Why, I had no trace of you for years!

MISS L. I suppose not.

STONOR. Very well, then. What *could* I do?

MISS L. Nothing. It was too late to do anything.

STONOR. It wasn't too late! You knew—*since* you "read the papers"—that my father died that same year. There was no longer any barrier between us.

MISS L. Oh yes, there was a barrier.

STONOR. Of your own making, then.

MISS L. I had my guilty share in it—but the barrier (*her voice trembles*)—the barrier was your *invention*.

STONOR. It was no "*invention*." If you had ever known my father——

MISS L. Oh, the echoes! The echoes! How often you used to say, *if* I "knew your father!" But you said, too (*lower*)—you called the greatest barrier by another name.

STONOR. What name?

MISS L. (*very low*). The child that was to come.

STONOR (*hastily*). That was before my father died. While I still hoped to get his consent.

MISS L. (*nods*). How the thought of that all-powerful personage used to terrorise me! What chance had a little unborn child against "the last of the great feudal lords," as you called him.

STONOR. You *know* the *child* would have stood between you and me!

MISS L. I know the *child* *did* stand between you and me!

STONOR (*with vague uneasiness*). It *did* stand——

MISS L. Happy mothers teach their children. *Mine* had to teach me.

STONOR. You talk as if——

MISS L. —teach me that a woman may do a thing for love's sake that shall kill love.

(*A silence.*)

STONOR (*fearing and putting from him fuller comprehension, rises with an air of finality*). You certainly made it plain you had no love left for me.

MISS L. I had need of it all for the child.

STONOR (*stares—comes closer, speaks hurriedly and very low*). Do you mean then that, after all—it lived?

MISS L. No; I mean that it was sacrificed. But it showed me no barrier is so impassable as the one a little child can raise.

STONOR (*a light dawning*). Was that why you was *that* why?

MISS L. (*nods, speechless a moment*). Day and night there it was!—between my thought of you and me. (*He sits again, staring at her.*) When I was most unhappy I would wake, thinking I heard it cry. It was my own crying I heard, but I seemed to have it in my arms. I suppose I was mad. I used to lie there in that lonely farmhouse pretending to hush it. It was so I hushed myself.

STONOR. I never knew——

MISS L. I didn't blame you. You couldn't risk being with me.

STONOR. You agreed that for both our sakes——

MISS L. Yes, you had to be very circumspect. You were so well known. Your autocratic father—your brilliant political future——

STONOR. Be fair. *Our* future—as I saw it then.

MISS L. Yes, it all hung on concealment. It must have looked quite simple to you. You didn't know that the ghost of a child that had never seen the light, the frail thing you meant to sweep aside and forget—*have* swept aside and forgotten—you didn't know it was strong enough to push you out of my life, (*Lower with an added intensity.*) It can do more. (*Leans over him and whispers.*) It can push that girl out. (STONOR'S *face changes.*) It can do more still.

STONOR. Are you threatening me?

MISS L. No, I am preparing you.

STONOR. For what?

MISS L. For the work that must be done. Either with *your help*—or *that girl's.*

(STONOR *lifts his eyes a moment.*)

MISS L. One of two things. Either her life, and all she has, given to this new service—or a Ransom, if I give her up to you.

STONOR. I see. A price. Well——?

MISS L. (*looks searchingly in his face, hesitates and shakes her head*). Even if I could trust you to pay—no, it would be a poor bargain to give her up for anything you could do.

STONOR (*rising*). In spite of your assumption—she may not be your tool.

MISS L. You are horribly afraid she is! But you are wrong. Don't think it's merely I that have got hold of Jean Dunbarton.

STONOR (*angrily*). Who else?

MISS L. The New Spirit that's abroad.

(STONOR *turns away with an exclamation and begins to pace, sentinel-like, up and down before* JEAN'S *door.*)

MISS L. How else should that inexperienced girl have felt the new loyalty and responded as she did?

STONOR (*under his breath*). "New" indeed—however little loyal.

MISS L. Loyal above all. But no newer than electricity was when it first lit up the world. It had been there since the world began—waiting to do away with the dark. *So has the thing you're fighting.*

STONOR (*his voice held down to its lowest register*). The thing I'm fighting is nothing more than one person's hold on a highly sensitive imagination. I consented to this interview with the hope—— (*A gesture of impotence.*) It only remains for me to show her your true motive is revenge.

MISS L. Once say that to her and you are lost!

(STONOR *motionless; his look is the look of a man who sees happiness slipping away.*)

MISS L. I know what it is that men fear. It even seems as if it must be through fear that your enlightenment will come. That is why I see a value in Jean Dunbarton far beyond her fortune.

(STONOR *lifts his eyes dully and fixes them on* VIDA'S *face.*)

MISS L. More than any girl I know—if I keep her from you—that gentle, inflexible creature could rouse in men the old half-superstitious fear——

STONOR. "Fear?" I believe you are mad.

MISS L. "Mad." "Unsexed." These are the words to-day. In the Middle Ages men cried out "Witch!" and burnt her—the woman who served no man's bed or board.

STONOR. You want to make that poor child believe——

MISS L. She sees for herself we've come to a place where we find there's a value in women apart from the value men see in them. You teach us not to look to you for some of the things we need most. If women must be freed by women, we have need of such as—(*her eyes go to* JEAN'S *door*)—who knows? She may be the new Joan of Arc.

STONOR (*aghast*). That *she* should be the sacrifice!

MISS L. You have taught us to look very calmly on the sacrifice of women. Men tell us in every tongue it's "a necessary evil."

(STONOR *stands rooted, staring at the ground.*)

MISS L. One girl's happiness—against a thing nobler than happiness for thousands—who can hesitate?—*Not Jean.*

STONOR. Good God! Can't you see that this crazed campaign you'd start her on—even if it's successful, it can only be so through the help of men? What excuse shall you make your own soul for not going straight to the goal?

MISS L. You think we wouldn't be glad to go straight to the goal?

STONOR. I do. I see you'd much rather punish me and see her revel in a morbid self-sacrifice.

MISS L. You say I want to punish you only because, like most men, you won't take the trouble to understand what we do want—or how determined we are to have it. You can't kill this new spirit among women. (*Going nearer.*) And you couldn't make a greater mistake than to think it finds a home only in the exceptional, or the unhappy. It's so strange,

Geoffrey, to see a man like you as much deluded as the Hyde Park loafers who say to Ernestine Blunt, "Who's hurt *your* feelings?" Why not realise (*going quite close to him*) this is a thing that goes deeper than personal experience? And yet (*lowering her voice and glancing at the door*), if you take only the narrowest personal view, a good deal depends on what you and I agree upon in the next five minutes.

STONOR (*bringing her farther away from the door*). You recommend my realising the larger issues. But in your ambition to attach that girl to the chariot wheels of "Progress," you quite ignore the fact that people fitter for such work—the men you look to enlist in the end—are ready waiting to give the thing a chance.

MISS L. Men are ready! What men?

STONOR (*avoiding her eyes, picking his words*). Women have themselves to blame that the question has grown so delicate that responsible people shrink—for the moment—from being implicated in it.

MISS L. We have seen the "shrinking."

STONOR. Without quoting any one else, I might point out that the New Antagonism seems to have blinded you to the small fact that I, for one, am not an opponent.

MISS L. The phrase *has* a familiar ring. We have heard it from four hundred and twenty others.

STONOR. I spoke, if I may say so, of some one who would count. Some one who can carry his party along with him—or risk a seat in the Cabinet.

MISS L. (*quickly*). Did you mean you are ready to do that?

STONOR. An hour ago I was.

MISS L. Ah! . . . an hour ago.

STONOR. Exactly. You don't understand men. They can be led. They can't be driven. Ten minutes before you came into the room I was ready to say I would throw in my political lot with this Reform.

MISS L. And now . . . ?

STONOR. Now you block my way by an attempt at coercion. By forcing my hand you give my adherence an air of bargain-driving for a personal end. Exactly the mistake of the ignorant agitators of your "Union," as you call it. You have a great deal to learn. This movement will go forward, not because of the agitation, but in spite of it. There are men in Parliament who would have been actively serving the Reform to-day . . as actively as so vast a constitutional change——

MISS L. (*smiles faintly*). And they haven't done it because——

STONOR. Because it would have put a premium on breaches of decent behaviour. (*He takes a crumpled piece of paper out of his pocket.*) Look here!

MISS L. (*flushes with excitement as she reads the telegram*). This is very good. I see only one objection.

STONOR. Objection!

MISS L. You haven't sent it.

STONOR. *That* is your fault.

MISS L. When did you write this?

STONOR. Just before you came in—when—— (*He glances at the door.*)

MISS L. Ah! It must have pleased Jean—that message. (*Offers him back the paper.*)

(STONOR *astonished at her yielding it up so lightly, and remembering* JEAN *had not so much as read it. He throws himself heavily into a chair and drops his head in his hands.*)

MISS L. I could drive a hard-and-fast bargain with you, but I think I won't. If *both* love and ambition urge you on, perhaps—— (*She gazes at the slack, hopeless figure with its sudden look of age—goes over silently and stands by his side.*) After all, life hasn't been quite fair to you——

(*He raises his heavy eyes.*)

You fall out of one ardent woman's dreams into another's.

STONOR. You may as well tell me—do you mean to—— ?

MISS L. To keep you and her apart? No.

STONOR (*for the first time tears come into his eyes. After a moment he holds out his hand*). What can I do for you?

(MISS LEVERING *shakes her head—speechless.*)

STONOR. For the real you. Not the Reformer, or the would-be politician—for the woman I so unwillingly hurt. (*As she turns away, struggling with her feeling, he lays a detaining hand on her arm.*) You may not believe it, but now that I understand, there is almost nothing I wouldn't do to right that old wrong.

MISS L. There's nothing to be done. You can never give me back my child.

STONOR (*at the anguish in* VIDA'S *face his own has changed*). Will that ghost give you no rest?

MISS L. Yes, oh, yes. I see life is nobler than I knew. There is work to do.

STONOR (*stopping her as she goes towards the folding doors*). Why should you think that it's only you, these ten years have taught something to? Why not *give* even a man credit for a will*ing*ness to learn something of life, and for being sorry—profoundly sorry—for the pain his instruction has cost others? You seem to think I've taken it all quite lightly. That's not fair. All my life, ever since you disappeared, the thought of you has hurt. I would *give* anything I possess to know you—were happy again.

MISS L. Oh, happiness!

STONOR (*significantly*). Why shouldn't you find it still.

MISS L. (*stares an instant*). I see! She couldn't help telling about Allen Trent—Lady John couldn't.

STONOR. You're one of the people the years have not taken from, but given more to. You are more than ever . . . You haven't lost your beauty.

MISS L. The gods saw it was so little effectual, it wasn't worth taking away. (*She stands looking out into the void.*) One woman's mishap?—what is that? A thing as trivial to the great world as it's sordid *in* most eyes. But the time has come when a woman may look about her, and say, "What general significance has my secret pain? Does it 'join on' to anything?" And I find it does. I'm no longer merely a woman who has stumbled on the way. I'm one (*she controls with difficulty the shake in her voice*) who has got up bruised and bleeding, wiped the dust from her hands and the tears from her face, and said to herself not merely, "Here's one luckless woman! but—here is a stone of stumbling to many. Let's see if it can't be moved out of other women's way." And she calls people to come and help. No mortal man, let alone a woman, *by herself*, can move that rock of offence. But (*with a sudden sombre flame of enthusiasm*) if many help, Geoffrey, the th*i*ng can be done.

STONOR (*looks at her with wondering pity*). Lord! how you care!

MISS L. (*touched by his moved face*). Don't be so sad. Shall I tell you a secret? Jean's ardent dreams needn't frighten you, if she has a child. *That*—from the beginning, it was not the strong arm—it was the weakest—the *little*, *little* arms that subdued the fiercest of us.

(STONOR *puts out a pitying hand uncertainly towards her. She does not take it, but speaks with great gentleness.*)

You will have other children, Geoffrey—for me there was to be only one. Well, well—(*she brushes her tears away*)—since men alone have tried and failed to make a decent world for the little children to live in—it's as well some of us are childless. (*Quietly taking up her hat and cloak.*) Yes, *we* are the ones who have no excuse for standing aloof from the fight.

STONOR. Vida!

MISS L. What?

STONOR. You've forgotten something. (*As she looks back he is signing the message.*) *This.*

(*She goes out silently with the "political dynamite" in her hand.*)

CURTAIN.

The Gresham Press,
UNWIN BROTHERS, LIMITED,
WOKING AND LONDON.